RIDING LIGHTNING

STARCROSSED DRAGONS BOOK 1

ERIN BEDFORD

J. A. CIPRIANO

Copyright © 2017 by Erin Bedford & J.A. Cipriano

All rights reserved.

No part of this book may be reproduced in any form or by any electronic or mechanical means, including information storage and retrieval systems, without written permission from the author, except for the use of brief quotations in a book review.

WANT TO GET FREE STUFF?

Sign up here. If you do, I'll send you some free short stories.

Visit Erin on Facebook or on the web at ErinBedford.com.

ALSO BY ERIN BEDFORD

∼

<u>The Underground</u>

Chasing Rabbits

Chasing Cats

Chasing Princes

Chasing Shadows

Chasing Hearts

∼

<u>Fairy Tale Bad Boys</u>

Hunter

Pirate

Thief

Mirror

Stepbrother

∼

The Celestial War Chronicles

Song of Blood and Fire

Visions of War and Water

∼

The Mary Wiles Chronicles

Marked By Hell

Bound By Hell

Deceived By Hell

Tempted By Hell

∼

The Crimson Fold

Until Midnight

∼

Vampire CEO

Granting Her Wish

ALSO BY J.A. CIPRIANO

Starcrossed Dragons

Riding Lightning

Grinding Frost

Swallowing Fire

Pounding Earth

∼

The Goddess Harem

The Tiger's Offer

The Wolf's Hunt

The Dragon's War

∼

Justice Squad

Miracle's Touch

∼

Her Angels

Heaven's Embrace

Heaven's A Beach

Heaven's Most Wanted

∼

The Shaman Queen's Harem

Ghosts and Grudges

1

We'd done it. It was right there on my screen in an interoffice memo. Waesigar, Realm of the Dragons, had sold more than thirty million copies on release day, making it the highest selling PC game to date. I should have been happy; all my other coworkers were celebrating in the other room. Their cheers and drunken banter could be heard even in my tiny cubicle. But my heart wasn't in it.

It had been easy enough to create this fantastical world that has everyone in such an uproar, but for them, it was just make-believe. Something they could indulge in to get away from the real world. But not me.

The hard-worn warriors of Waesigar who could

transform into glorious beasts with wingspans as large as semi-trucks weren't just code in a computer to me. Those beasts were real. As real as the long cold cup of coffee on my desk and just as hard to digest.

I'd left home to get away from the dragon world and all that it entailed. Sadly though, the human dimension required one to have skills I hadn't learned from my long line of royal tutors or from training with the guard. Humans might think being a dragon was cool, but there was so much more to it than flying around breathing fire.

For one, my family, well, all the dragon world really, focused on providing an heir, something I'd never had much interest in. It made being banished a blessing in some ways. I could date who I wanted and have children or not. It was completely up to me.

Secondly, dragons tend to be all about strength and dominance. If you weren't a big muscly warrior, you didn't have much of a say in anything. Which my father attested to by being the one who made all the decisions. If my father knew I'd become a software engineer, he'd probably have a heart attack.

Sure, it hadn't been on my list of dream jobs. Heck, it hadn't even been on my mind until I started talking to my now best friend, Ryan, about Waesigar. He, of course, thought it was some story I had fabricated and suggested I go into writing, but the creative arts didn't exactly pay the bills. At least, not right away. A far safer choice had been to hone my skills in the IT industry.

It'd been pure luck when Ryan and I had both gotten an internship at the prestigious Mist Game Corp. He mentioned my story to another coworker, and they passed it to another. Before long, my story had gotten to the head of game development, and as they say, the rest was history.

"So, this is where you've been hiding, Maya." Ryan came around the corner, out of breath like he had been jogging. The more likely culprit would be the karaoke machine the company had rented for our release party.

Ryan had a lean build not from working out but from being blessed with a fast metabolism. Something he groaned about day in and day out. It made me want to gouge his eyes out with as he called it 'my freakishly sharp claws.' They weren't really claws, not like my kind's dragon form, but they stayed long and hard without much upkeep. I only wished the rest of me took so little effort to maintain.

I spun around in my chair with my hands in the air and plastered a small smile on my lips. "You caught me. I'm a party pooper."

"What's up?" Coming completely into my five by five cube, Ryan leaned against the built-in desk. He crossed his arms over his chest, drawing my eye to the Waesigar promotional t-shirt with its swirling reds and golds, the same as my family's crest, emblazoned on the fabric. My heart clenched at the sight.

Get a hold of yourself, Maya. I deliberately shook the longing which had griped at me since the countdown to release day had begun. My home had been easy enough to put out of my mind before I'd started this project. Now, though? Now I saw it in every poster, every video on the web. It almost made me wish I could go back home.

I gave Ryan a watery smile and shrugged. "Oh, nothing. Just feeling homesick. I wished I could talk to my family at a time like this."

Ryan offered me an understanding nod, "Must be hard being so far from your family. They live in India, right?"

"Yeah," I agreed, the lie falling off my tongue

so easily after all this time of repeating it. Ryan was my closest friend, and I wished I could tell him everything. Only how could I tell him my family really resided in another dimension? I might as well buy myself a one-way ticket to the looney bin.

"Well, you can call them later." Ryan bumped me on the shoulder with a lopsided grin, "I'm sure they wouldn't want you moping in here by yourself when there is perfectly good *free* booze being served in the other room."

I lifted a brow at Ryan's temptation. He knew I didn't drink. Not because I didn't want to, but because it didn't really have much effect on me. Dragon's Tears, the alcohol of choice back in Waesigar, had a bigger bite than a double shot of bourbon and that was considered the cheap stuff. So, when others asked, I just said I didn't drink and left it at that.

"Fine." Ryan rolled his eyes, "All the *free* soda you could possibly want. Now come on, don't make me use my mad karate skills on you." He held his hands up and made chopping motions along with fake martial arts sounds.

I laughed and grabbed his hands, "Okay, okay. Stop before you hurt yourself, Master Ryan."

"Master Ryan," he paused, tapping a finger on his face. "I like this sound of that."

"Oh great. Don't go getting a big head." I chuckled following him out of my cube and toward the sound of the party. From the high-pitched cawing, my manager, Margarete, was trying to sing a country love song again and butchering it.

"I think this will be one of those nights where you wished you drank." Ryan winced as Margarete hit a particularly high note.

I forced myself not to put my hands over my ears even though Margarete's off-key voice was agony to my enhanced hearing. I had to agree with him. This was going to be one long stone cold sober night.

∼

THREE A.M. WAS NOT a time I enjoyed in Waesigar or on Earth. I liked it even less since my ears were still ringing from hours of listening to my drunk coworkers destroy any chance I'd ever want to listen to music ever again. I had finally been able to make my excuses and sneak out of the party just as they were talking about getting tacos. Like they hadn't had enough food at work?

My keys jangled as I stood before my apartment door. My eyes were heavy, and my back ached from all the limbo I was conned into paying so I didn't notice my door was already partially open until I tried to put the key into the hole. The door pushed open, and I stumbled through catching myself before I fell to the ground.

I froze mid-bend. Someone was in the room. My eyes darted along the floor, my nostrils flaring as I took in the changes to the apartment. It was subtle, but the usual mix of cinnamon and last night's takeout had a new odor added to it. Like spicy chocolate. I cocked my head to the side as I realized the scent was familiar.

"I could have killed you ten different ways in the time it has taken you to recognize me," the deep baritone called to me from my living room.

Frowning, I straightened my bent form. My emerald eyes met dark gold as I came face to face with Ned, my father's first lieutenant. Lounging on my couch with either arm thrown over the back of the cushions, his large, bulky form took up most of the sitting space.

I pushed my dark hair back from my face with a huff, irritated at being taken off guard. "What are you doing here?"

"Now, is that any way to talk to your favorite cousin?" Ned stood from the couch, his sword clanging against his side. He wore Waesigaran armor, a deep red leather infused with our own dragon scales. It took a lot of energy and training to shift into our full dragon forms, and only the strongest were able to sustain it for long periods of time, let alone long enough to pull off their own scales for use as armor. Having dragon scales on our armor symbolized our strength in the eyes of our opponents. Ned had almost a full chest plate of them.

Walking into the living room, I scanned the area for any other unexpected visitors. Satisfied he was alone, I dropped to the ground, sweeping my leg out and hitting Ned in the back of the knees. He slammed into the ground, a grunt exploding from his mouth. I leapt back to my feet and smirked down at him.

"I might not have a full armory at my disposal here, but the humans have other ways to train." Holding a hand out to him, I helped my cousin back to his feet as he grinned.

"Good." He took a deep breath, evidently still recovering from my attack. "I'd hate to report to your father that his daughter had become soft."

"Pfft." I waved him off and headed for the kitchen. "Like he could be bothered with me. I haven't heard from him in five years why should he care now?" I busied myself by making a pot of coffee. Like alcohol, caffeine didn't have much of an effect on me, but if I was going to have this conversation, I'd need some kind of stimulant.

"You know why he hasn't," Ned said from behind me having followed me into the kitchen. My apartment wasn't huge, but it had plenty of counter space, and I liked that. Having grown up with chefs most of my life, I found learning to cook for myself both empowering and a soothing practice.

"Doesn't matter." I shook my head, closing down the line of conversation. I didn't want to rehash my father's decision to send me away while my older sister, Aeis, acted as heir to Waesigar. She'd always been more powerful than me. Hell, she had achieved her wings at the age of fifteen. I was just over twenty-five and still haven't been able to grow mine. Not for the lack of trying, sadly. Most dragons came into their wings around puberty, but mine seemed to be defective. Or maybe it was just me. I could see how the Lord of Western Waesigar would choose her over me.

"It does matter." Ned stepped up next to me.

"Your father loves you. He didn't shut you out like you think."

"Could have fooled me," I muttered as I poured myself a cup of coffee and then added a heavy dose of sugar and milk. While the drink might help me stay awake, the taste of it still reminded me of the tar pits in the Outlands, an area in Waesigar where no one went unless they had a death wish. Thinking about it made me wonder why I even bothered to drink the damned stuff.

"My father's affections aside you still haven't told me what you are doing here and at three in the morning." I gestured with my cup at the microwave clock. I glanced down at my cup and then to Ned. "I'd offer you some, but I know you wouldn't take it."

Ned's eyes glanced down to my cup and his lip curled in disgust. "I don't know how you have survived on that drivel all these years. The stuff humans call food is vile."

"You get used to it." I shrugged, drinking from my cup.

"I'm here to retrieve you," Ned finally answered. He crossed his arms over his chest and leaned against the counter as if waiting for me to overreact. Well, I wasn't about to give him the satisfaction.

Swallowing a mouthful of sweetened caffeine, I poured the rest of my cup down the sink. Rinsing it out, I put it in the drainer to be used again. Then without saying a word, I walked past Ned and into the living room.

The light on my answering machine blinked, alerting me to a message. I'd been told most people didn't have house phones anymore, but I didn't like the idea of someone being able to track me. Five years in the human world and some habits never changed.

I pushed the button to play the message while acutely aware of Ned following me once more. Ignoring him, I focused on the voice coming out of the machine.

A high-pitched squeal that made me wince was followed by the giggling of my other best friend, Bianca. I'd met her in an art class while in earning my degree. I'd never thought I'd become friends with such a woman. Someone who shopped more than she breathed and always ragged on me to dress more girly. I could hardly tell her that compared to some of the females back home, I was considered small for my size and my rounded face made me more adorable than fierce. I didn't need to dress in frilly clothes to make me seem feminine, my features did it for me. One of my greater flaws in the eye of my father.

A Waesigar princess was beautiful, fierce, and above all in control. To the court and my father, I was none of those things. Not like Aeis with her curvy figure and cool reserve. She rarely raised her voice and always knew exactly how to act in every situation. How I missed her.

Bianca's loud nasally voice knocked me out of my thoughts and back into the now.

"Congratulations, biatch!" Bianca howled into the machine. "We are definitely going out for drinks tomorrow night. You're buying. Or you better be with that big raise you are getting! Anyways, I'll see you tomorrow at the normal place, eight o'clock, and *no* pants. We're going to get you laid if I have to do it myself!"

I quickly shut the machine off with a groan. The likelihood Ned hadn't heard that last part was probably as likely as the Northern Ice Lands had become a balmy paradise since I'd been gone.

"At least, you have not been sullying yourself with the males of this world," My cousin growled coming up behind me. The alpha in him had come out to play, and my dodging would no longer be allowed.

"Well," I gave a short laugh and turned around to face him, "what can I say, I'm picky." That wasn't completely true. I just didn't have much interest in finding a mate.

"Which will serve you well in picking a mate." His mouth formed a stern line as he towered over my short frame, making me feel even smaller than I was. Had he gotten taller in the last few minutes?

"Picking a mate?" I squeaked not sure I had heard him right.

"Yes," Ned nodded, "I have come to take you home. It is your time to choose a mate and provide an heir for your kingdom."

My mouth dropped open, and I shook my head in disbelief. "No. There has to be some kind of mistake. I was sent to this dimension because I wasn't worthy enough to mate, remember?" I raised my brows at him. "Aeis is the heir, not me. My genes are not worthy of leading our people." I recited back the words my own father had said to me on the day my sister was announced as the next heir.

"Things have changed," Ned said his eyes softening.

Getting mad at Ned wouldn't help things. After all, he had been one of the few who had tried to fight my father for me. One of the only ones, actually. My mother was so far under my father's thumb she wouldn't dare question him in private let alone in front of the whole Western Court. If my brother hadn't died four months before he would have stood up for me, but as it was, we were all too wounded by the loss for me to have brought it up at that time. Even now, part of me was glad I hadn't, even though if I had, maybe I wouldn't have had to leave the only home I knew and relearn everything in the human world.

"Well, I don't care!" I spat, anger suddenly gripping me. "He wanted to banish me so I wouldn't try to take the kingdom away from his precious Aeis. He can't just change his mind whenever he wants." I stomped away from Ned and back into the center of the living room. "If you haven't noticed, I've made a life for myself here. No thanks to him. Dumping me here without anyone to direct me, he might as well have sent me to the Outlands."

"And that is exactly why we need you back." Ned gestured around the quaint apartment, "You've made a home, found employment and friends in a world you didn't know. Without anyone to guide you, you have thrived all on your own. Waesigar is in turbulent times." He shook his head sadly. "We need someone like you to help calm the fires."

I forced myself not to snort at the imagery. Then I asked the one question which had been bugging me since Ned arrived. "What about Aeis? She's who you all wanted, the one fit to rule. Are you just going to toss her aside? Maybe send her here in my place?" I waved my arms around the room wildly.

"No," Ned answered in a calm voice which caused my anger to cool a bit. "There is no need to cast her out. She's no threat."

A heavy feeling settled in my throat, and it bobbed up and down as I asked, "Ned, what happened to Aeis? Why are you really here?"

Ned's eyes fell to the ground, and he sighed miserably. "Your sister is alive and well but has been found barren."

I gasped, my hands going to my mouth. As dragon shifters, it was hard enough to have children. Most shifters couldn't carry the child to term without shifting in some aspect, and doing so caused so much stress on the body, the child often didn't survive. But being barren? It was a fate worse than death to our people. Having a child was everything. Even more so than making sure the child was from a strong and worthy bloodline. It was no wonder Ned was here.

"So," I said, trying to keep the bitterness from filling my voice, "it's not that you need my ability to survive, it's that you have no one else." I shook my head angrily. "I did exactly what my father thought I would, and I'm not even there." Delirious laughter left my lips, and before I realized it, I was giggling until my stomach hurt and tears ran down my face.

"I wished there was some other way, Maya, I really do." Ned approached me, placing his hands on my shaking shoulders. "Still, the reason for your return doesn't matter. I believe this is a blessing for our people. I wasn't lying when I said we needed you. Too long have our people focused on strength and tradition. It has caused many of the troubles we are having now. Things will never change if we do not start at the throne."

While I sympathized with Ned, I didn't really see how that had anything to do with me. Sure, I was the only remaining royal child of the Western Lands, but that didn't mean I could fix them. I could provide an heir to keep our line going, but that didn't mean anything would change. Nevertheless, my opinion didn't have much value. Whether I wanted to go or not, my father would find some way to get me back to Waesigar and doing what he wanted, regardless.

Wiping my face with the backs of my hands, I breathed a deep sigh. "I guess I don't really have much of a choice, now do I?"

"No, not really," Ned apologized, and oddly enough, I knew he meant it.

"Fine." I pulled away from his embrace before I broke down again. "But I'll need to get some things. Call some people."

I couldn't just pick up and disappear without a trace. I had too many people here who would start to wonder where I went. Bianca and Ryan would move hell and high water to find me if I didn't leave them word. I'd also need to let my job know I was going on personal leave and hope I still had a job when I came back. *If* I came back.

Starting to gather my things, I settled a depressed look at the answering machine. I guess I wouldn't be getting drinks with Bianca after all.

2

"I can't believe you are leaving me!" Bianca cried out from the couch where she had thrown herself in an act of despair. "Who am I going to go shopping with?"

"I don't go shopping with you now," I pointed out before shoving a few more things into the bag Ned had reluctantly allowed me to bring. When Bianca and Ryan came over my cousin had made himself scarce, which I was thankful for. No need to explain what he was doing here or why he was dressed up like a character from the video game I'd just helped create.

"But you could if you were here to try!" Bianca jerked her arms out in front of her in an over-exaggerated manner.

Ryan chuckled as he came out of the kitchen. He'd been pretty quiet since I told him. Only nodding his head as I tried to explain my sudden need to go home. We had just talked about it yesterday, so maybe he'd been a bit more prepared than Bianca.

"She's not dying." Ryan sat down in the only other chair in my living room. "You should put yourself in Maya's shoes. She hasn't seen her family in how long? Four years?"

"Five," I corrected, holding my hand up and displaying all five of my fingers like a toddler who had just learned to count.

"Exactly." He jerked his head back to Bianca, "Your family lives in town. Hers lives in a completely different country. Imagine how that would feel?"

Bianca chewed on her lip, her mouth turned down in a frown. "I would hate it. I couldn't fathom not having Sunday brunch with all my siblings or seeing my parents. You must feel horrible." She jumped up from the couch and wrapped her arms around me in a tight hug. "I'm so sorry I tried to make this all about me."

"Don't worry about it." I patted her back with a small smile. Even if Bianca could be a drama queen, I couldn't ask for a better friend. It almost made me wish I was bringing her to Waesigar. There I'd always been the lesser dragon, so my friends had been in short supplies.

I took a step away from her and looked at my two friends. "I'll be back before you know it. You won't even have time to replace me."

"Ha!" Bianca snorted. "Who could replace you?"

"Right." Ryan stood and walked over to join in our group hug. "There's no way we'd even dream of it. Besides, you have to come back to help make Waesigar 2. The higher-ups are already talking about expansion packs!"

I laughed at Ryan's enthusiasm. He really had landed his dream job working at Mist. While I enjoyed my job, it was just a means to an end. I guess part of me always thought I'd end up going back to Waesigar. Even as I found myself fighting it.

There was just one problem though. What was I really gaining by going back?

Not a whole hell of a lot. My father would keep our family in control of the Western Lands like he always wanted. The kingdom would get an heir. And I would get what? A child and a mate I would be duty bound to stand by?

"All right, alright." I dropped my arms to end the hug. "I still have to finish packing and talk to my landlord. So, you crazies need to get out of here before I change my mind."

"Well, in that case…" Bianca started with a grin.

"Out." I pointed a finger toward the door with a shake of my head. Though I smiled, my throat threatened to close from fighting back the tears. I forced them back until I closed the door on them and the little life I'd made for myself here.

I took a deep breath as I collapsed against it, back pressing against the cheap wood, and gave myself a moment to lament the loss of my life. Unshed tears slid down my face, and I let myself wallow for a moment in my fate.

Alright, that's enough, I thought and rubbed the tears from my face. This was no time to fall apart. I'd go with Ned without a fight because I had little doubt he would drag me kicking and screaming if he had to.

Besides, I really wanted to stand in front of my father and tell the bastard I had no desire to rule or be his little brood mare. The look on his face would make everything worth it. Or at least I hoped it would be.

Pushing off the door, I went about packing. It was hard to choose what to take and what to leave. After all, there was always the chance I wouldn't come back. How was I supposed to choose what to leave behind?

In the end, I decided to take things which had sentimental value. Some pictures of Ryan, Bianca, and me, a baseball cap from my very first game, and a handful of books from my favorite authors. I wanted to share them with Aeis since she shared my love of reading.

A sudden thought came to me, would my mate love to read? Would I even like him? I didn't dare hope to love him because, in the end, it didn't come down to love, it came down to who could get me pregnant. With any luck, I'd be lucky enough to tolerate him.

Sighing at my own dark thoughts, I zipped my bag just as Ned came back in the apartment.

"Are you ready?" His eyes settled on my bag. "Is that all you wish to take?"

My eyes downcast, I struggled with the need to take more, but after a moment, I turned to my cousin. "I'm ready."

Getting to Waesigar wasn't something one could easily do. There was no taking the train or a crowded plane ride. Waesigar resided in another dimension entirely, which could only be entered by way of a portal. But there were rules about creating portals and not just anyone could make them. Ned apparently had the authority, or he wouldn't have been the one to retrieve me.

"Is this really where you've picked to summon a portal?" I asked, looking around the empty parking garage. It had been a few blocks away and was jam-packed with cars, but since everyone else was working, it was empty of people.

"This is where the ley lines are strongest," Ned said, raising an eyebrow at me. He gestured around the parking garage. "We could have gone somewhere closer, but you insisted on talking to your friends, so we missed a chance at opening others."

"Fine," I said, remembering how that conversation had gone. Oddly, enough, the argument with my cousin had been easier than I'd expected. Maybe it was because he felt bad for me? I wasn't sure, but either way, I appreciated it. "Thank you, by the way."

"For what?" he asked, meeting my eyes with a

look of uncertainty. It struck me as odd because my cousin was always the picture of confidence.

"For letting me tell my friends goodbye." I held up my small travel bag. "And for letting me take some things."

He looked at me for a long time before nodding. "You're welcome." For a moment, it seemed like he'd say more, but instead, he just lifted his hand and muttered a spell under his breath.

Sparks of eerie green light leapt from his fingertips, leaving glowing contrails in the air as he shoved his hand against the very air itself. The reality before him tore, splitting open to reveal a pulsating rip in the fabric of space and time. With a grunt, he grabbed onto the ragged edges of the portal and jerked it violently sideways, widening the opening until it was large enough for us to pass through.

"You've gotten better at that," I commented as he lowered his hand. I'd never been able to create a portal. I could levitate objects and even close my curtains with a swish of my hand, but the ability to create portals was well beyond my skill level.

"I know." Ned gave me a confident grin before gesturing forward in a mock bow. "After you, Your Highness."

My lips twisted into a grimace at the title. Five

years without it, and I couldn't say I missed it. Nor all the responsibilities which came with it.

When I didn't move, Ned straightened, his eyes trained on me. "Stalling will only cause to anger your father. We are already a day behind schedule as it is."

"What? Did he expect me to drop everything and come running? Like a good little lap dog?" When Ned stayed quiet I scoffed, "He did, didn't he? Not that I should be surprised. He always thought his wants were so much more important than anyone else's." I sighed and then pushed my shoulders back. This was a pointless argument, and we both knew it. "Well, then let's get this over with."

Before Ned could say anything else, I stepped through the portal. The magic swirled around me tingling along my skin. There was a brief moment where my body was pulled in two different directions – not a painful feeling more like pressure – before I left earthly dimension and entered the dragon world.

The darkened sky of Northern Waesigar greeted me with its twinkling lights, giving me the first reminder of the differences between this world and Earth. I'd left Earth around three o'clock in the afternoon, but based on the moon's position in the sky, it was late evening here.

My family's castle stood before me. The portal had taken me to the outskirts of the palace. We were at the back gate the servants usually took. It seemed my father didn't wish to publicly announce my return.

I felt Ned step through the portal before I heard him, and as I turned to look at my cousin, he gave me a slight smile and moved to stand next to me. He breathed in deeply as if the air on Earth had been mediocre in comparison and placed a hand on my shoulder. "Welcome back to Waesigar."

His words made my stomach sink. I was really back home. I remembered all the nights I had claimed I wouldn't come back even if they begged me. That I'd rather chew off my hand before I stepped foot in Waesigar again. Yet, here I was, doing the very thing I had promised I would never do. The sudden urge to turn around and run back to Earth hit me like a kick in the teeth.

Ned's hand tightened on my shoulder as if he could read my thoughts. I swallowed hard and forced myself not to move. Evidently, that satisfied him because he dropped his hand and started forward. When I didn't immediately follow, Ned twisted around to look at me. "Come, you cannot stay out here all night. Your father wishes to introduce you to your suitors."

My mouth dropped open, and I stuttered as I caught up with him, "Suitors? As in more than one? He couldn't possibly already have someone picked out for me. He didn't even know I would come back."

Ned made a disgusted noise in the back of his throat. "Your father is nothing if not confident in his ability to control those around him. You should be grateful he is even giving you a choice. The two males he has chosen for you to meet are both good matches and would do your kingdom proud."

I could just imagine what that meant for my suitors. Probably large boorish males who cared nothing for intelligence and all for brute strength. Besides, I was pretty sure that despite what Ned said, if my father had picked them, they weren't for me.

Still, I had to admit, part of me was curious. My father would choose the best. Not because he cared anything for me, but because he wouldn't want weak offspring. With any luck, that meant they'd at least be nice to look at. A small consolation, I know, but hey, it was something, right?

Ned led me through the gates and into the palace. I received a few curious looks from passing servants. Probably more because of my odd clothing than my being there. The jeans and gaming t-shirt were not something even the lowliest of servants would be dressed in. Most dressed in what earthlings would consider upper middle-class clothing. My family had a penchant for suits and full-length gowns. I shuddered at the thought.

"Your old room has been cleaned, and clothing has been provided for you," Ned told me though I hadn't asked. He must have noticed the looks we were getting as well.

"I've grown since I've been here last," I couldn't help saying, purposely being difficult.

"I'm sure you will make do, but if nothing fits, I will have a tailor summoned." When I didn't reply, Ned became silent. I followed behind him down a corridor and up a flight of stairs until we finally reached my room.

I stared up at the double metal doors. They were the same as before. Ned pushed the door open to reveal the room within. It too was the same. My four-poster bed was covered in a dark red duvet. The large wooden wardrobe I used to hide in as a child stood against one wall. The rug where I'd spent countless hours reading still lay in the middle of the room. I wondered if it was still as soft as I remembered.

"I'll leave you to change." Ned gestured around the room before turning to the door. He paused at the frame and gave me a warning glance. "Your father will want to see you, so don't leave him waiting longer than need be."

As the door shut behind him, I stuck my tongue out. Childish? Yes. But it made me feel better.

I tossed my bag on the bed and gave in to my curiosity. Taking my shoes off, I let my toes sink into the rug. Yep, exactly like I remembered.

So soft, it was like stepping on a cloud, and for a moment, I almost contemplated taking a nap on it. As I knelt down to run my hands over the threads, a knock came to my door. I sat up, startled, and as I turned to look, it swung open to reveal my sister, Aeis.

"Maya!" Aeis cried out, her full mouth curved into a delighted smile. She was dressed in a floor-length cream-colored gown which exposed her shoulders, and she moved across the room with such grace she seemed to float.

"Aeis," I almost sighed. For all my sister's faults and my father's favoritism, I still loved her. It was hard not to. We might be different in every way but just seeing her made a part of me relax. All thoughts of sleeping on the rug flew from my mind as my sister raced toward me. I let myself be engulfed in her embrace, my dragon practically purred from the familiar scent of family.

After a moment, Aeis spoke. "I didn't think you would come."

"Father didn't really leave me a choice." I frowned and pulled out of her arms. Matching emerald eyes met mine as we both assessed the other. She, probably because of the length of time apart, me because I was sure I'd never see her again after I'd last talked to father.

"You've changed, Maya," Aeis concluded, dropping my gaze and circling around me like a vulture. "One would hardly think you were one of us now."

I shrugged, not wanting to get into what I had to do to become what I was now. "I adapted."

Aeis frowned, her brow furrowed in concentration. "I'm sure you have, but father will not be pleased with your changes. We will need to postpone the meeting of your suitors until I have had time to get you cleaned up."

Though I should have been offended, I could have kissed her. Any chance to stave off meeting father and his suitors was a blessing to me. It took everything in me to look contrite and not bursting with joy as I murmured, "If you think so."

"Don't even pretend to be upset," Aeis snorted, crossing her arms over her chest, "You might have been gone, but that doesn't mean you will suddenly be able to pull one over me. I'm still your sister." Aeis smirked and headed for the door.

"Aeis." I stopped her before she could leave. "I'm really sorry about—"

"Don't worry about it," Aeis cut me off with a sad smile. "These things can't be helped. In any case, father can wait until you are presentable. I'll be back in the morning to help you prepare." She started to leave but stopped. "Maya, I'm just really happy you are back."

"Me too," I answered as she shut the door behind her. With her words still ringing in my ears, the reality of my situation crashed down on me, reminding me I wasn't here by choice. No matter how much I wished otherwise.

To try to get my mind off the impending doom that was my father, I decided to see if my favorite garden was still intact. I creaked the bedroom door open, half-expecting a guard in front of it. With the hallway utterly deserted, I wasted no time hurrying down it, in case someone tried to stop me.

Each familiar turn down the stone corridor made my heart beat faster. The same tapestries lined the walls, the same mixture of sulfur and cobblestone filled the air. Panic and excitement caused my pace to quicken until I almost sprinted down the halls.

I would have kept running until I arrived at my destination had it not been for the brick wall I slammed into as I turned the corner. My feet came out from under me, and I braced myself for the impact of the hard floor, but it never came. A large, warm hand grabbed my arm, jerking me away from the inevitable pain and into the most delicious scent I'd ever smelled.

Rain and thunder. It filled every cell of my senses making it hard to breathe and my body to react in the most erotic way. The creature holding me inhaled deeply, and a growl rumbled through his chest and my nipples hardened in response.

Embarrassed by my reaction to my savior, I eased away from him. My eyes met a strong jawline and a crooked grin. That grin alone caused things to become slick between my thighs. My dragon wanted him. No, that wasn't quite right. After all these years away, it needed him in a way I couldn't explain.

I swallowed thickly, licking my lips as I took in his olive complexion and dark eyes. They crinkled at the sides but at the same time bore into my soul.

"Why hello there," he said playfully.

"Uh, hi," I squeaked and shook my head. Stepping away from him, I cleared my throat and wrapped my arms around my middle, "I mean, sorry. I wasn't looking where I was going."

"Don't worry about it." He chuckled, running a hand through his short dark hair, the ends of them tipped white. "You'll hear no complaints from me. Feel free to run into me anytime."

"Heh heh, okay." I ducked my head down and glanced up at him beneath my lashes. What was wrong with me all of a sudden? Have I been away from my kind for so long that the first male I come across makes me turn into a cat in heat? I didn't react that way to Ned, but then again, he was my cousin.

During my internal war, my savior had closed the distance between us, his scent overwhelming my system once more. I gasped and backed up a step my back pressing against the wall beside us. He braced his hands on either side of my head, and for a moment I thought he might kiss me, but his head dipped down bypassing my lips and burying into my neck.

My eyes fluttered closed as his nose trailed along the line of my neck, my breathing coming in ragged pants. We weren't touching anywhere important, but with his nose pressed against my throat, we might as well have been screwing given the effect it had on my body. The place between my thighs pulsated and ached to be touched. A mewling sound escaped my mouth and my hips arched to find some kind of release, but the moment I pressed against the hard front of his pants, he jerked away from me.

The heat of his body disappeared, leaving me cold and wanting. My eyes shot open, and I found myself utterly alone. What the hell was that?

In a desire filled haze, I made my way back to my room, no longer interested in the garden. I didn't bother undressing as I slid into bed, my head full of rain and thunder. Who was he?

3

The time difference didn't make it any harder to fall asleep. With the little sleep I'd had the night before and all that had happened in such a short time, my body was ready to pass out.

So, when Aeis pulled the curtains aside early the next morning, I couldn't help but groan in displeasure. I shoved my pillow over my head to block out the light, but my sister was having none of that.

"Come on now, you can't sleep all day." She tugged the covers off of me, and I pulled my legs and arms into myself curling into a ball for defense.

"You slept in your clothes?" Aeis made a noise of disgust as her presence moved away from the bed.

"It was a long night," I croaked, peeking up from underneath the pillow. Aeis opened the wardrobe and flipped through the clothes that had been picked out for me. From my spot on the bed, I could make out enough to know my father hadn't picked them. There wasn't a frill or bow in sight.

"You know," she withdrew a long burgundy gown and studied it for a moment before laying it on the bed, "if father had his way, you'd be laid out naked on a platter with nothing but bows covering your bits. And maybe not even the bows." She frowned and stared off into the distance like she was imagining that very scenario. "For some reason, he doesn't think any suitor will want you without being distracted by your body first."

Eyes narrowed, I crawled out of bed with a raging fury. "Fine, I get it. I'm not the ideal candidate for this position, but he's the one who demanded I come back, not the other way around!"

"And that is precisely why we are going prove him wrong," she gestured for me to disrobe, and while I wasn't sure what her plan was exactly, I complied. If there was one person I could trust in Waesigar, it was Aeis.

"Fine," I muttered, stripping off my clothes and

standing there in front of her in just my undergarments.

Aeis looked me up and down, a sly smile on her lips. "At least, you have filled out a bit in the places that matter."

Placing my hands on my hips, I growled, "I'm so happy you approve."

"Don't take your anger at father out on me. I'm just following orders." She held her hands up in defense before going over to the bathroom door. Ducking inside, she came back out with a washcloth and a comb. "We don't have time for you to bathe fully so this will have to do."

Grimacing, I took the cloth from her and proceeded to wash my face and all the other important parts. Aeis worked on my hair, twisting it this way and that until it was bound in a long braid down my back and decorated with an ornate comb. When she was satisfied, I slid the dress over my body and let it settle over my shoulders and cling to my hips.

"There, that's better," Aeis said, rubbing her chin between her thumb and forefinger. "You can hardly tell you've been gone."

"Banished you mean."

Aeis rolled her eyes. "Semantics."

"Not semantics," I snapped, spinning around. "Let's not forget what this is. I'm only here to provide an heir, and I wouldn't even be that if you could have children." A cloud of sadness covered Aeis's face, and guilt filled me. "Oh God, Aeis. I'm sorry. I didn't mean it."

"No, you're right. No need to pretend this is something that it's not." She gave me a half-hearted shrug.

"But I shouldn't have made it sound like it was your fault." I shook my head, feeling worse and worse about how I'd acted. "I know how much being a mother and the heir meant to you. Much more than it ever meant to me."

Aeis smiled softly. "It'll become important to you too. Just wait, you'll see."

I opened my mouth to tell her not to hold her breath but stopped when at the hesitant knock on my door. We both turned as the door opened to reveal my mother Lanays, Queen of Northern Waesigar.

Her eyes were the same shade as mine, but her hair had more of an auburn color to it like our brother, Ricon's. Unlike, Ricon's, hers was streaked white. Time had not been good to her. Her face had gained several lines since I'd been gone. But when she saw me all that didn't matter. Her face lit up, and she looked years younger.

Without a word, I rushed into her arms. Burying my face in her hair, I inhaled deeply. Home. She smelled of home.

"Maya, my daughter," she murmured in my ear, her hand stroking my back and hair while being careful to avoid the metal clip. "I never thought I would see you again."

"Well, I'm here now. Let's go see these suitors father has lined up for me." I leaned back from her with a smile. I hadn't realized how much I had missed my mother until right then. I could have all the friends in the world but nothing compared to being with one's mother.

"I think they'll be quite surprised," my mother said right before she licked her thumb and rubbed a smudge on my cheek. "You're just positively radiant." My chest warmed at her words, but another part was embarrassed by her gesture. I wasn't a dragonling anymore.

"Mom," I said, ducking away, but before I could, she snagged my arm.

"Oh, come now. Can't a mother have some fun?" she chided as Aeis took my other arm. "Now let's go. Everyone has waited quite a long time, and while I'm sure the boys will think it was worth the wait, your father won't."

On that cheery note, my mother and Aeis led me down the corridor. "Many things have happened since you've been gone."

"Oh really?" I asked, cocking my head to the side. "Ned said something along those lines as well."

"Yes," my mother added. "Your father and the other lords, unfortunately, are repeating the mistakes of their forefathers."

"What do you mean?" I turned to her, watching her face for any clues to what they were talking about, but my mother would put a statue to shame with how guarded her expression was.

My mother pressed her lips into a thin line seeming to think on what to tell me, then after a moment, she stopped Aeis and me from going any further. "Your father, while I love him dearly, still believes that brawn before brains is the answer. He'd die before trying to talk through his issues with the other lords. We've already had more than a dozen raids in the last year, and we have had enough."

"So, what am I supposed to do about it?" I placed my hands on my hips. They didn't know what they were talking about. I'd never been the one with the answers or even someone who could persuade others to my side. More often than not, they had already decided what they thought about me after the first meeting. Which I hoped my family would see sooner rather than later. "I couldn't make him listen when I was here before why should he now?"

"Because," Aeis placed her hand on my arm, "once you have produced an heir, you'll have all the power. You and your new mate will make the rules. No more raids. No more hit first and talk later."

What Aeis said made sense but - boy, were they barking up the wrong tree. I couldn't lead anyone let alone a whole kingdom. It would only be a matter of time before they realized it and banished me back to Earth once more. Part of me wanted to make them figure it out sooner rather than later, but the other half missed home and wanted to stay as long as possible. Hard to know what to do when I didn't know myself.

We stopped in front of the entry to the throne room where my suitors and my father no doubt waited. I dropped their arms and took a step back.

"Maybe we should do this later?" I glanced between the two of them, anxiety building up inside of me. "I haven't even eaten breakfast yet. I can't meet my suitors on an empty stomach." I placed my hand on my stomach and gave a nervous smile.

Obviously seeing through my façade, Aeis stepped forward and took my hand. "Everything will be fine. You act as if you're about to be thrown into a pit of snakes. You're not. You're meeting two strapping men just dying to make your acquaintance."

"I doubt that," I grumbled, letting her bring me toward the entry once more. Holding onto Aeis's hand tightly, I tried not to vomit as all my nerves and worry threatened to come flying out of my mouth.

Unlike the rest of the palace, the throne room had changed. There used to be an intimidating throne at the top of the room, one in which I had cowered before on more than on occasion, but now three smaller chairs sat where it once was. I could only assume they were meant for my mother, sister, and I.

As I glanced around the wide-open space of the throne room which was usually filled with nobles and soldiers, I only saw three people. My father stood at the head of the room, his gray hair, which used to be a dark brown, caught my eye immediately. Hands behind his back, he spoke in a low voice with the two other occupants.

The taller of the two had long silver hair pulled back in a ponytail. His shoulders were stiff, and his hands were behind his back mimicking my father's posture. The other one had a familiar head of dark hair with white tips, and the sight of him made my stomach sink.

"Ah." My father's face lit up as he saw us. "Here she is now."

At my father's announcement, the two backs turned, and my sinking feeling was fully realized. Dressed in a pale-yellow shirt, my eyes instantly went to the long span of skin showing where several buttons were undone. Hands tucked in his pockets, they were barely big enough to hold him let alone his hands and I half wished he'd turn around so I could see the effect on his backside. When my eyes finally landed on his face, his familiar knowing grin made me swallow hard.

The sexy, playful male I'd met last night was one of my suitors. There was a twinkle in his eyes which made me think he knew exactly who he had accosted in the hallway. I'd been virtual putty in his hands all while he took advantage of my ignorance.

"Maya," my father called to me, gesturing for

me to come forward. As I approached, he wrapped an arm around my shoulders in a side hug. I didn't get the same sense of home from him as I did from my mother. I forced myself not to tense against his touch, but I wasn't able to make myself smile. I wasn't that good of an actress.

"It's good to see you back in these walls." There was a warning in his tone, which was hard to miss. "Where you belong."

Lips pressed into a thin line, I replied, "It's good to be back." Before he could draw out the home warming, I turned my attention to the men in front of us. "Can I correctly assume you are my father's choices for my future mate?"

"Yes," my father unfortunately answered for them giving me a bit of a nudge forward. "This," he gestured to the male with white hair and a cool expression on his handsome face, "is Jack from the Northern Area. He comes highly recommended by his cousin, Vincent, who as you may remember, is the High Lord of the Frozen Mountains."

Jack, an odd name for a dragon, and it didn't exactly match the composed demeanor of the male in front of me. His eyes were pale almost translucent except for the hint of blue as they caught the light. Through his perfectly tailored suit, I could tell he had a nice build, but something about him gave me the impression he might be more of a politician than a fighter. There was an ethereal beauty to him, but the stony expression on his face left me wary.

An awkward silence filled the room when I didn't take a step toward him but thankfully, Jack seemed to know what to do. Holding his palm out to me, I placed my tanned hand into his pale one, the contrast of my warm temperature to the coolness of his a bit of a shock to my system. Even more so when he bent at the waist brushing his lips against the back of my hand.

As soon as I was able, I snatched my hand back and fought back the need to rub it against my skirt. My skin tingled from where his mouth had touched me. Before I could think more on the tingle racing through me, I turned my attention to my other suitor.

The moment my eyes settled on the white-tipped male, he stepped forward into my personal space. The scent of rain and thunder filled my senses, and once again my body reacted to his overwhelming maleness. I pressed my thighs together, trying to stave off the need while standing in front of my family.

"We've actually already met," the white tipped

male said, looking at my father who had been about to introduce him. Unlike Jack, this guy definitely didn't feel the need to be a gentleman. Something I found both alluring and annoying. He turned his gaze to me. "Haven't we?" His eyes twinkled mischievously as he wrapped his arms around my waist, pulling my body against his own while pressing his lips to my cheek. Warmth ran through me from where his lips touched my skin and landed straight between my thighs. Damn. These guys were going to make it hard to be annoyed about the whole forced mating thing.

"What is he talking about?" my father asked, jerking myself out of my daydream. His expression was hard to read, I couldn't tell if he was angry or not. I also didn't know whether I really cared because my entire focus was on the man holding me. Still, I was a princess, and I couldn't let this guy think he could manhandle me any way he pleased even if, right now, that was exactly what my inner dragon wanted.

I pushed away from his embrace even though my dragon screamed in protest. Then, even though I didn't know why, I turned toward Jack. "We ran into each other in the hallway last night. He was just as forward then." I rolled my eyes. "Perhaps he could take a cue from you." I glanced back at Mr. White-tips. "Common courtesy is to introduce yourself first."

"Raiden," my mysterious male answered with a cheeky grin. "My name is Raiden. Third son of the King of the Eastern Region."

"Raiden." I let the name roll off my tongue while giving him a warning look. What I did now would direct the course of our entire relationship, and given our circumstances, that might be a long one indeed. I had to let him know he couldn't use his sexy to get what he wanted. I mean, it'd probably work for now, but in a few weeks when my dragon wasn't so hot and bothered, it'd likely just piss me off.

"Such a pretentious name," Jack muttered under his breath, and when I glanced his way, I found him smiling very slightly like there was a joke only he got. Hmm... maybe there was more to him than I'd initially suspected.

"Pretentious?" Raiden said with a laugh while glancing over at Jack. "You're named Jack. That's the most boring name I could ever think of." He gestured at Jack with one hand. "Guess it fits you."

Before Jack could reply, I stepped between them, hands raised. "It's nice to meet you both."

Only, it didn't seem like either had heard me. They were too busy glaring daggers at each other. It was a little weird because I knew part of the reason for their rivalry was because of me, and honestly, I'd never been in a situation quite like this. I took a deep breath, trying to think of what I could possibly say when Aeis placed a hand on my arm.

"Well," Aeis smiled at my suitors, "I don't know about you men, but I am famished. Why don't we head to the dining room for breakfast?" She giggled slightly. "I bet you two can eat a lot."

Aeis always knew how to dissolve the tension. Usually, I'd have gotten irritated, but in this situation, I was grateful. I mouthed a thank you as their tension dissolved and they turned to look at my sister.

"That is an excellent idea," my father said, and there was a touch of sadness to his voice. Just that one sentence let me know he was even more upset with my being here than he had been before. The thing was, I sort of agreed. Aeis was definitely better suited to rule than me. Part of that wasn't my fault though, after all, I'd been gone forever while she'd been preparing to take over. Of course, she'd be better at it.

Besides, feeling sorry for myself wouldn't help

the situation. No, I had to learn and learn fast. As we made our way to the dining room, I dropped back, sidling up to my sister and leaning close. "Can I chat with you afterward?"

"Of course," she whispered back, giving me a knowing smile.

"Thanks," I said as we entered the dining room.

"Take your seat," my father said, gesturing at the spot between Jack and Raiden.

Aeis squeezed my hand as I nodded to my father. "As you wish," I mumbled, moving forward.

As I went to sit down, Jack pulled my chair out for me. As I settled in my seat, I turned to thank him, but before I could, Raiden's thigh pressed against the side of mine, drawing my attention. He shot me a grin as if daring me to say something. I should have been angry at him. For last night, for teasing me now, but all my body could think about was how he had felt when he had me pressed against the hallway wall. Instead of responding, I turned back to Jack.

"Thank you," I said before focusing on the plate in front of me with only one thought running through my mind.

I was screwed.

4

In the history of dinners, this had to be the worst yet. Currently wedged between my possible future mates, one I already found myself wanting to make long hot love to and the other — well, I wasn't quite sure about it.

What I did know was my parents and sister being there only made matters more awkward. Maybe not my sister, she was usually good for defusing a situation, but my father's over-excited grin as he tried to play matchmaker made my stomach roll. Who knew he was so eager to pimp out his daughter.

"So, Raiden," my sister paused to take a drink from her cup, "you have two other brothers, correct?"

Raiden's eyes lit up at the mention of his brothers. "Yes, Aido and Dreq."

"What are they doing while you are here?" Aeis asked while I pushed my breakfast around on my plate.

"Oh, probably crawling over each other in their quest for my father's favor." He laughed and threw his arm over the back of my chair.

My shoulders tensed as his arm pressed against the back of my neck. The rest of the table's occupants didn't seem bothered by Raiden's boundary issues. Except maybe Jack who had a frown on his lips. Though, that might be for a number of reasons.

"So, why aren't you trying for the throne?" I turned in my seat so Raiden's arm would slip off of me. The more he touched me, the less my brain seemed to function properly.

He shot me a smirk that caused all kinds of hot tingles to go through me as he readjusted himself. "I was never known to be the studious kind. I've always been more interested in the sensual arts." He licked his lips, his eyes devouring me in one quick movement that made the skin on my chest burn and the place between my thighs slicken and throb.

"Then what makes you think you are worthy of

the Western Lord's daughter?" Everyone's attention jerked around to the solemn dragon, Jack. His expression had hardly changed, but a tiny clench of his jaw showed me he had been paying more attention than I had given him credit for. Not so aloof after all. Interesting.

While everyone else turned to look at Jack, I kept my eyes on Raiden. That was an answer I wanted to hear. The thing was, Raiden didn't seem bothered by the question.

"I might not have been the best student, not like my brothers were, but I still know my way around a political gathering." His grin widened. "And, more importantly, no can beat me in hand to hand combat." The confidence in his voice left no room for argument. There was a bite to it though which caused me to squirm as if he might punish me if I dared to argue. I had a feeling any punishment he dished out would be worth it

"As am I," Jack replied the challenge clear in his voice. The two males locked eyes, and for a second, I wondered if they'd fight over me here and now. It was a bit strange for me because while I'd never been the girl guys fought over, I sort of liked the idea of it. Oh God, how sad was that?

"That's wonderful," my father said, clapping his

hands and breaking the tension. "Both of you are far more than worthy to mate with my daughter. Better still, there will be plenty of chances for each of you to prove your worthiness."

"And how exactly would they do that?" Brow furrowed, I frowned at my father. "Aren't you just going to tie me down in a room and let them both fuck me a few times until I'm good and seeded?" I shrugged. "You know, find out who the father is afterward as it has been for millennia." I waved my hand dismissively.

My father's grin became feral. "You didn't really think this would be like your sister's mating, did you?" He shook his head, and as he was about to say more, I interrupted.

"I wouldn't know, I wasn't here," I snapped returning his grin with a vicious one of my own.

His expression dropped, and for a split second, I could see guilt color his eyes. Well, that was new. I hadn't expected the bastard to feel bad about banishing his youngest daughter.

Mother and Aeis stared down at their plates not saying anything but apparently, not everyone in the room knew the score. Jack's face hadn't changed much, but he did look at me in question. Raiden wasted no time voicing his opinion.

"Why weren't you here?" His brow bunched together genuine curiosity on his face. "I know you were away studying, but surely you'd have returned for that?"

Laughter rolled from my lips, a deep belly laugh which had nothing to do with joy and everything to do with the bitter disdain I held for the man who created me.

"You couldn't even man up to it could you?" I snarled at my father whose face colored a deep purplish red.

"I am afraid I am in the dark on this one as well. Would you care to elaborate?" Jack said, his cool gaze fixing on my father.

"Yes, Lord Dannan," Raiden's attention focused on the head of the table, "I, too, wish to know why exactly I haven't been able to meet the lovely Maya before now?" He shot me a lascivious look. "She's positively delicious."

My face warmed at Raiden's question. I had only meant to put my father on the spot, not draw more attention to myself. I pushed my delight in Raiden aside and focused on my father, wondering if he would finally fess up to being in the wrong. Admittedly, I didn't have high hopes.

"Well, I..." the Western Lord stumbled over his

words under the intense look the visiting males were giving him. I knew he wanted to lie on the spot, but no doubt the scrutiny made it more difficult, especially since he likely hadn't prepared to have this fight in front of our guests. No, he'd expected me to kowtow to him just like everyone else. As his eyes darted to my mother and sister, neither of whom offered him any help, I almost laughed. From the look on their faces, they seemed to enjoy seeing him squirm.

Unfortunately, my father's unbalance didn't last long. "Maya was indeed studying abroad." My father cleared his throat and straightened in his seat. "In fact, she is the first of our kind of have earned a degree in the human dimension. This was all part of my plan to make her an even more valuable asset to any lucky enough to mate with her." He ended his explanation with a warning glare as if daring me to contradict him otherwise.

I should have known he wouldn't tell the truth. At least, not the whole truth. Still, that he knew I had a degree surprised me, but then again, he had twisted it around, so I sounded like a better catch than I was. Maybe that had been his plan ever since retrieving me. To use everything, I'd done on my own to sell me to one of these two. It seemed like it had worked too. My potential mates seemed thoroughly impressed though.

"Whoa." Raiden's mouth dropped open. "You were in the human dimension? What was it like? Do they still lack the basic knowledge of the mystic arts?"

My father relaxed in his seat having firmly turned the attention away from him and back onto me. Jack sat forward in his seat as if he too wanted to know more about the human dimension. Sighing at the lack of justice in the world, I nodded. "Yes, their idea of magic includes machines and pyrotechnics. If you even brought up magic, they'd think you are going to do some card trick or pull a rabbit out of a hat."

Raiden laughed, smacking the table with his hand. "What? Why would anyone want to do that?"

My lips curled up slightly at his amusement. "It's their form of entertainment."

"They seem to be quite the unintelligible barbarians," Jack commented, taking a drink from his glass. "I couldn't imagine you learned much from them."

Frowning at his assessment, I twisted to face him. "Quite the opposite actually. They have many inventions we don't have, and even with their lack of magical ability, they've advanced further than one could imagine in the medical field."

Having spent five years with the so-called barbaric humans, it was only normal I'd be a bit defensive. Especially since, when Jack insulted the humans, I couldn't help but think he was talking about Bianca and Ryan. A pang of longing hit me so suddenly, my throat burned. I reached for my glass but missed, knocking it over and spilling the contents across the table and onto Raiden's lap.

Jumping up, Raiden tried to wipe the liquid off of his pants without much success. I grabbed my cloth napkin, and without thinking, bent down, rubbing at the wet spot on his pants. I realized too late that had been the wrong thing to do. As my hand pressed against his hardness, Raiden released a startled noise.

Jerking my hand away, my eyes went from his lap and up to his face where his eyes had hooded in desire and his mouth had gone slightly slack. A clearing of the throat pulled my gaze away from him, and I straightened scooting back into my seat. I kept my eyes down on my plate not daring to look anyone at the table in the eyes. I couldn't believe how impulsive I had been.

First, I'd gone from arguing about the humans,

and then I'd practically sexually assaulted one of our guests right in front of my whole family. God, could this day get any worse?

"Father," my sister, ever the goddess, drew the attention away from me, "you were talking about something you wanted them to do? Maybe you could explain that now?"

"Ah, yes. Thank you for reminding me," my father said, nodding sagely.

While I was highly interested in what he planned for my potential mates and me, I couldn't find the courage to take my eyes off my plate for more than an instant. To be totally honest, I'd have been pretty damned happy if the floor opened up and swallowed me just then.

"While you two are wooing my daughter, you will also be tested on your ability to work as a unit." Jack and Raiden shifted next to me as if to hear my father more clearly. So far it didn't sound like anything I would want to do. Then again, why did I ever think it would be?

"How will we do this?" Jack asked his voice even and analytical as ever. "We are competing against one another."

My father cleared his throat as if prepared to give a long-winded speech. "As many of you know,

Waesigar hasn't been in the best of times. There is quite a bit of conflict between our lands about how we should rule."

His words reminded me of Ned's and my sister's warnings from before. They were deeply worried about the dragons keeping too focused on tradition. This must be what they were talking about.

"So," my father continued, "I am tasking you three to go to the Southern Mountains and get their lord to reaffirm our alliance."

"Why can't you just send a messenger?" I asked, slightly confused. That would be what we'd normally do. Sending the three of us was most unusual.

My father's jaw tightened, and his hands gripped the table in front of him. A petty part of me enjoyed how my questions were bothering him. "Because they have yet to answer any of my messengers, and I, myself, cannot travel to their lands where they might be waiting to attack."

"But we can." I jumped in, causing my father to shoot daggers at me with his eyes.

"I have little doubt you are proficient enough to stay out of trouble and with your two strapping escorts." He nodded to Raiden and Jack. "You will have no trouble getting there, and hopefully you can use some of their political experience to come to some kind of agreement with the Lord Amun."

"Do not worry, Lord Dannan," Jack spoke calmly with his hands folded in front of him. "I will take personal responsibility for your daughter's safety and secure this alliance for you. I have no doubt I shall prove the better match for her."

I forced myself not to roll my eyes at Jack's proclamation and then jumped in place as Raiden's hand came down on my inner thigh. Glancing up at Raiden's almond-colored eyes, I couldn't help but blush.

"While our companion is focused on politics," Raiden murmured into my ear as Jack and my father discussed the particulars of the journey. "I will be more than delighted to adhere to your every need." Each word was enunciated with a slight squeeze to my thigh that sent a scorching heat between my thighs.

"I'm sure you will." I licked my lips and glanced up at him beneath lowered lashes. If this man could affect me so easily in a room full of people, I couldn't imagine how hard it would be to keep away when we were alone.

"Maya." Jack's voice reminded me we wouldn't

be completely alone on this trip, which I was only partially thankful for.

"Yes?" I asked, pushing Raiden's hand away.

"Would you like to leave today or would you rather spend more time with your family first?" Jack questioned with a raise of his brow.

It was such an insightful question I almost didn't know what to say.

Thinking about it for a moment, I searched myself for the answer. Did I really want to spend more time with my family? The answer was instantly a yes, which was the problem. If I spent more time with my sister and mother, I would become attached to them again. That would make it even harder for me to leave them. If not impossible.

No. The best thing for everyone would be for me to find a way out of this and head back to the human dimension as fast as possible. Getting pregnant wasn't in my plan. I had a life back on Earth, and while it might not be anything as extravagant as being a dragon princess, I had every intention of getting back to it.

"While I appreciate your concern for my feelings, I think it would be best to get started right away." I glanced at my father before continuing, "If what I've heard is true, even one more day might be too late. We don't want another war to occur. We all lost so much during the last one."

My father nodded his approval as my sister and mother's faces fell. It almost made me want to change my mind, but I steeled my back and stood from the table. "I should go prepare for the journey. If you would excuse me." I pushed my chair back as Jack and Raiden stood from theirs. Before either of them could offer to escort me, I darted away from the table and into the hallway.

I wasn't quick enough, however, because my father stopped me by calling my name. Spinning around, I found him standing there in front of me.

He placed his hands on my shoulders with a proud expression, something I'd never seen in my entire life, and part of me was annoyed at how good that made me feel. "You are handling this better than I imagined, Maya. I trust I can count on you to do the right thing here?"

"I don't know what you mean?" I cocked my head to the side, genuinely confused.

He sighed and ran a hand over his face, "Look, we both know you weren't my first choice, but you are our only hope now. So, don't screw this up. We need an heir no matter what. I trust you will be able to do what you have to do to accomplish that?"

I stared at him hard for a moment, his words not quite clicking. Then my mouth dropped open. "Wait, you want me to do both of them?"

"Now, I didn't say that." My father held his hands up. "I'm just saying if one doesn't get the job done, feel free to take advantage of your options." He patted me on the shoulder with a surprisingly genuine smile. "I know you will make me proud."

Nodding, I turned away from him and stepped out of the room. My father's words played over and over again in my mind. Dragons weren't monogamous in most cases unless they were from high families. Since getting pregnant was hard enough, a lot of females had more than one mate, but I had never thought I would be one of them, let alone, have my father suggest it.

I shook my head in disbelief. What was the world coming to?

5

I'd been searching through the clothing my sister had picked out for me, hoping to find something suitable for our quest for the last hour and a half. It was doubly frustrating because my drawers were filled with frilly dresses, which, while pretty, wouldn't work for where my father expected us to go.

Southern Waesigar was barely more than a volcano. How the dragons who called the place home managed to live in the barely inhabitable desert was beyond me. Then again, we couldn't all live in rolling plains and endless trees, and as I contemplated the journey ahead, I had to admit my father had gotten the better home.

"None of this is going to work," I huffed,

throwing another dress to the side and glaring at it angrily. "Is there even one pair of pants in the lot?" I stood there for a moment longer before deciding I'd need to find a seamstress myself and get some proper attire.

I stomped across the room and flung it open to find Raiden standing there, one hand raised as though he'd been about to knock.

"Hey." Raiden smirked at me and leaned against the door frame, causing the gap in the collar of his shirt to expose his muscular chest.

"Can I help you?" I quirked a brow at him, trying not to press my thighs together in an effort to ease the sudden need tingling there.

Eyes crinkling at the corners, Raiden peered into my room over my shoulder and smiled, "Need help packing?"

"Not really." The absolute last thing I needed right now was to let the nearly irresistible dragon into my bedroom. Sure, it might start out innocently, but once we were alone, well, let's just say I was worried about keeping my hands and mouth to myself. Behind closed doors with a bed so close? I doubted we'd leave for our quest anytime soon.

"Are you sure?" he asked again, taking a step closer and peering past me into the room. The movement caused his muscular chest to brush against my breasts. An electric shock went through me, and as a small sound escaped my throat, my inner dragon screamed at me to close the distance even more. No. Not just that. It wanted me to tear off his clothes, to wrap my naked body around his, to let him take us as his own.

I shut my eyes, trying to fight off the insatiable need of my inner dragon, and as she railed against me with years of pent-up need, Raiden's scent filled my nostrils.

Rain and thunder.

A growl slipped from my throat and heat pooled between my thighs. Before I could so much as blink, Raiden's hands were around my waist, pulling me against him as his mouth found mine. He had boasted of his strength and agility not more than an hour ago, and as he effortlessly backed me into the bedroom, I believed it.

My inner dragon and I moaned in unison as the taste of him filled our mouth. My hands buried themselves in his dark locks as I pulled him closer to us. He devoured me, not giving me an inch as one hand slid to the back of my neck while his other hand snaked down, cupping my left breast.

A gasp ripped from me that allowed Raiden to

travel from my mouth and to the junction of my throat. The hand at the back of my neck gripped my hair, forcing my head back to give him better access. I didn't mind though because my own fingers were too busy finding the edges of his shirt. With one sharp tug, I ripped it open, popping buttons free and tearing fabric. Then my hands were on the hard-strong muscles beneath. My nails dug into the warm skin of his chest causing him to hiss and pull back slightly.

Our eyes met for a moment, serving only to ignite the desire within me further. I inhaled sharply. The room smelled of lust and sex even though we hadn't taken our clothes off yet, and as my dragon relished in the taste of it in the air, I pulled him further into my room.

He wrapped his arms around me then, twisting us around, so his back was toward my bed as he buried his face in my breasts. The feel of his lips on the tops of my breasts sent a sizzle through me, and before I knew what I was doing, I'd pushed him backward. His knees hit the frame, and he fell flat on his back.

I looked down at him, my eyes raking over the bare muscle of his chest and felt my lips twist into a smile. Flat on his back, he watched me with hooded eyes as I lifted my skirt. I crawled over his legs until I straddled him. The press of his hardness against my heat caused us both to groan, and it took everything in me not to rock against him like my inner dragon wanted me to because I had something different in mind.

Locking eyes with Raiden, I slipped my arms out of my dress and pushed it down to my waist. The dress my sister had picked out for me this morning didn't allow for a bra with its low, wide neck, so when it came off my breasts were bared to the room.

Instead of reaching up, Raiden's hands gripped on my waist, empowering me and urging me to go one step further. Leaning forward, I let my breasts brush against his bare chest. A surge of pleasure exploded through me, shocking my senses and making me gasp.

I swallowed hard, trying to regain my bearings. I wanted to take this slow, and if this kept up, I'd just tear the rest of Raiden's clothes off and have my way with him. I didn't want that. At least not yet.

Instead, I placed each hand on either side of his face. Lowering mine down to his, I licked across his mouth and teased, "Is this the kind of help you were offering?"

"No, actually," his voice came out a low growl, "but I'm always happy to help a lady in need." To iterate his point, his hands pressed on my hips while he thrust against me.

With only my panties against his pants, every inch of him touched my sensitive mound, hard and more than ready for me. While I didn't plan on mating with either of the males my father had chosen for me, nothing was stopping me from having a little fun. My inner dragon agreed wholeheartedly, and as I stared down at Raiden's naked chest, I ground into him.

A strangled cry spilled from my lips as my mouth sought out his. Raiden helped my hips find a rhythm, his hands moving to squeeze my ass while thrusting against me again.

As our tongues tangled, a growl leaked out from our kiss. When the pressure began to build, and my legs started to waver, Raiden took control. Only instead of flipping us over like most alphas would have done, he kept me on top, finding just the right spot to make me scream.

Eventually, the pressure became too much, and it became impossible to concentrate on kissing him.

I shut my eyes as wave after wave of pleasure rushed through me. I moaned, driving myself against him as my peak approached.

"Oh yes..." I cried right before he stopped.

My eyes ripped open, and I stared down at a grinning Raiden. "What the hell?" I snarled, and when he only grinned wider at me, I tried to climb off him.

This time though, Raiden wasn't against showing me who was in charge. He held onto my waist while I tried to get away, suddenly embarrassed I'd let it get this far and angry I hadn't been able to finish. When he didn't budge, I glared down at him.

"Is this some sort of sick game to you?"

"No, actually it's not," Raiden said in all seriousness though his eyes still laughed at me, "but what kind of dragon would I be to let your first orgasm with me come from dry humping on your bed with the door wide open."

I gasped and twisted around slightly to see the door to the bedroom was indeed still open. I struggled with a renewed vigor to get off him and right myself. This time he didn't stop me from getting off, but instead of allowing me to climb off the bed he grabbed hold of my arms and pinned me face down to the bed with my butt in the air.

"What the hell are you doing?" I cried out, tugging on my wrists in frustration partially from his actions and partially because I was so turned on.

"Giving you what you want of course," he chuckled as he flipped my skirt over my back, exposing my panties to the room. His fingers slipped between my thighs rubbing against my slick heat. I tried not to cry out and buried my face in the mattress. His digits moved back and forth enough to make me squirm but not enough to give me what I really wanted.

When a jerk on the back of my panties caused a tearing sound, the cool air of the room against my heated parts causing me to shudder.

"Wait, the door." I gasped, not believing I was letting him touch me so. But it seemed all my good sense went out the window the moment my lips pressed against his.

"So?" he asked as if it didn't bother him at all. His fingers found me again and turned my objection into a high-pitched whine. He rubbed his hand against me, not entering but torturing me slowly until I was begging for release.

"You have two options, Maya," he said his

breath hot on my skin, "I can stop here. I'll leave, and you can close the door where you will no doubt have to finish yourself or..." he trailed off while rubbing circles around my most sensitive part. "Or I can give you what you really want."

I didn't answer at first because I was too engrossed on the way he made my body quake with desire, but as I pushed against him, his hand stopped once more, leaving me on the verge of tears.

"I'm waiting for your answer," Raiden commanded in a tone I hadn't expected from what I had seen of his personality. Up until this point, he'd seemed like all fun and games, no responsibility, no rules. Clearly, I'd pegged him wrong.

He had me wrong too. I wasn't like my mother or sister who could be easily brought into submission. I would not rely on a man to give me what I wanted. I'd always taken it. Which was what I tried to do next. Too caught up in the feelings he was causing my dragon, wouldn't let me think about what I was doing. I'd been dead set against mating with either of the suitors, but my mind was overridden by my need. I pushed my hips back, seeking the fingers which had stilled against me only to be met with a hard swat on my ass.

I gasped as a stinging sensation spread throughout my cheek.

"I asked you a question," he growled, his hand on my wrists tugging a bit harder. "Now, the longer you delay, the more likely someone will come by and see you in such a position." His hand on my backside slid down to dip between my thighs once more, making me moan. "I, for one, enjoy seeing you like this, but I'm not so sure your father and mother would. Do you?"

"No." I croaked out as his fingers moved faster against me once more. When he brought me to the edge again, I thought I wouldn't have to answer, but just before I reached it, he slapped his hand down hard on my ass once more.

"You still haven't answered my question, Maya. If you make me ask again, I will take you right here where anyone can see, and I will not stop until I've had my fill."

His threat caused my own dragon to roar in response, my vision became sharper, and I knew my eyes had shifted in anger. Gnashing my teeth as I turned my head to glare at him, "Do it. If you think you are dragon enough."

Raiden gave me a fanged toothed grin. His own eyes shifting to a golden hue, but instead of taking me like he had claimed he would, he let go of my arms. His face disappeared between my thighs. His tongue replaced his fingers, and my hands ripped at the covers in an attempt to hold on. I'd been brought to the edge so many times already that it only took a few swipes from him before I shouted my release.

Breathing heavily into the bed, I didn't even move to cover myself as he pulled away from me. His hands caressed my backside once more before my skirts were back down where they belonged. The bed shifted his weight no longer on it. I thought maybe he was coming around to make me return the favor, but instead, I heard the door close.

A mixture of irritation and confusion spilled through me. I'd definitely pinned him as a selfish kind of guy. The "give to get" kind of type. But here he had just driven me to the point of insanity and hadn't sought his release in return. What kind of man does that?

A crazy one, that's who, I answered myself.

6

Packing took way longer than I planned. Mainly because I couldn't cool down enough to face everyone. Especially, Raiden.

Just thinking of him made my body heat, and my cheeks hurt from smiling. Who knew someone with such a carefree personality could be so domineering in the bedroom? And the way he made me feel? I'd never felt anything so intense before in my life.

Not that I had a whole lot of experience.

My father wasn't the only one who saw me as lesser in the dragon world. The majority of the populace thought the same way. Even during the royal parties, I often found myself alone or hanging out with family members like Ned.

Still, now that I thought about it, there had been one person I'd met during one of those parties. He hadn't cared about my faults. In fact, he found them refreshing.

Firestar.

He had stood out amongst the rest, a large mountain of a man with hair of fire eyes so intense they burned straight through me. One quirk of his lips, and I had nearly fallen for him.

My heart momentarily warmed at the memory before filling with pain. Sure, we'd had three passionate nights before it had all ended, but ended, it had.

At the end of the summit, I had introduced him to my father. That had been a mistake. My father had been dead set against it. Said he was a hot-headed brute, and he'd die before he saw me mate with one of his kind. I'd never found out exactly what he'd meant, but Firestar was gone within the hour, and I'd been banished shortly after.

I shook my head.

Why was I even thinking of him now? Probably because I didn't have anyone else to compare to Raiden.

I let out a loud sigh.

"That doesn't sound good," Aeis commented from my side. I glanced up from where I had been unpacking and repacking my bag. The concerned expression on her face vanished as she stepped into the bedroom. Her nostrils flared, and she tilted her head up slightly sniffing the air.

"It's not what you think!" I shook my hands in front of me, my voice going up in pitch and making me sound even guiltier.

"And what is it that I think?" My sister cocked a curious brow as she walked across the room with her hands folded in front of her.

"That I already picked a mate?" I offered weakly but then quickly added, "Which I haven't, not yet."

"Then Raiden's scent in your bedroom is here because?" She stopped by the bed and wrinkled her nose, the scent of what Raiden and I had done no doubt reaching her nose. "Did you…?"

"No!" I cried out and then stared down at the floor as my face filled with heat. "I mean, no we didn't do that."

"But you did do something," she accused, I glanced up long enough to see the amusement etched on her face before my eyes shot back down to studying the floorboards.

"Yes, we did. I mean," I huffed and groaned in defeat. "It just happened. He was there, and he smelled so good, and it has been sooo long. I don't know what happened."

Aeis placed a hand on my shoulder and gave it a small, reassuring pat. "You don't have to explain yourself to me. Remember I've been in your shoes. Except I didn't have quite the drama your mating seems to have." I glared at her as she let out a laugh.

"Did something like this happen to you?" The uncertainty clear in my voice. I couldn't be the only one who had gotten overwhelmed before. Normally I would never let someone do that to me where anyone could have walked in. At least, I was pretty sure I wouldn't.

"Well, I'm not exactly sure what happened, to tell you if it was the same thing." Her brow furrowed as my heart leapt into my throat.

"Um, I…" I stumbled over my words and licked my lips, "I didn't act like myself. I was so… so —"

"Wanton?" my sister filled in for me, and I shyly nodded. "Oh, don't worry about that. All of us are like that."

"Really?" Hope raised in me at her words. The first good news I'd heard since this whole ordeal started. Maybe what happened to me with Raiden wasn't so bad then. "So, you let your mate do things to you that you'd normally never think of doing?"

Her lips pressed together into a thin line, "Well, no. Not that."

Crap.

"But I did feel out of control of my body and hormones," she added quickly, no doubt because of the expression on my face. "Like I was this big pulsating organ of need and the only way to have a moment of peace was to get pounded like a nail."

The expression on my sister's face mixed with her animated hand gestures made me burst out laughing. I held my stomach as giggles racked me, tears threatening to run down my face.

"Hey, you asked," Aeis giggled, placing a hand over her mouth as a blush spread across her cheeks. After a moment she sobered, her voice becoming serious. "In all honesty, you should be happy you are attracted to your suitor. It took weeks before I felt anything for mine."

Her admission made my laughter die. Confusion bellowed inside of me as I realized I had been so absorbed with my own problems, I hadn't even thought about what Aeis was going through. Hell, I hadn't even seen her mate at all since I'd gotten here.

"Aeis," I started slowly, "what happened? I mean, no one has even mentioned him at all."

A guarded expression came over Aeis's face, and I suddenly wished I hadn't asked.

"Gale," she sighed and rubbed a hand over her face, "he was a good man, a good dragon, but when we found out I couldn't have children, it became too much for him."

"And father just let him leave?" I scoffed in disbelief. "I hardly believe that."

"What was he supposed to do?" Aeis shrugged with a sad smile, "No one could blame Gale. Our numbers are becoming lower each and every day. If he had a chance to produce a child with someone else, it was in his right to do so."

"But," my mouth dropped open slightly, not accepting what she was saying, "I know most of us aren't monogamous, but he could have at least stayed around."

"Would you want to?" She shot me a look.

I sighed and shook my head, "No, I guess not. But that doesn't mean it was right."

"Anyways," Aeis grabbed my bag and tossed it

to me, "enough about my sappy story. This is your time. You have two more than worthy males to choose from, one you already know you could mate with. What are you going to do?"

Chewing on my bottom lip, I contemplated her words. What was I going to do? Raiden and I had so much chemistry, it would be easy to just announce him as my mate and get it over with.

Yet, I didn't belong here anymore, not really. I'd made a whole life back on Earth and leaving it all behind for something which my father clearly didn't want me to be a part of before wasn't right. So, my only chance to leave would be to drag this out as long as possible. Then when the time was right, I could find someone to open a portal back to Earth, and I would be back where I belonged.

"I'm going to see this through," I told Aeis. Part of me hated lying to her, but she had been through too much already. Telling her I didn't plan on staying would be cruel. Besides, I didn't know if I could handle another goodbye.

"And you are going to wear that?" She nodded her head toward the outfit I had chosen. Tight breeches that easily tucked into my boots and a loosely fitted tan short-sleeved shirt.

"What else would I wear?" I arched a brow. The

options hadn't been the best pickings. It seemed more like my wardrobe was meant for a mistress. Then again, I was supposed to be seducing a mate.

"You could have picked something a bit more feminine." She smoothed the edge of my collar and brushed my hair behind my ear. "I mean, this is practical, but not really what I had in mind."

I shrugged away from her, tossing the handle of my bag over my shoulder. "Well, I'm not changing. So they'll just have to fall for me like this. Or not at all."

"I suppose you're right. From the way they've both been looking at you, I'm pretty sure I could dress you in a parka, but that's hardly the point." Aeis sighed as we made our way out of my bedroom and down the corridor.

"It isn't?" I asked, but I didn't hear her response because with each step closer to the meeting spot I took, the more nervous I became. Raiden would be there. Would he say anything about what we did? Oh God, how was I supposed to act around him? Did he expect me to treat him differently now?

Then Jack's face came to mind. His beautiful stoic face made my palms sweat. Would he know what I did? Should I tell him? I didn't exactly understand the process of this whole situation.

Especially, since I wasn't going to pick Raiden right away.

Double crap.

My feet felt heavy as we approached the waiting group at the back of the palace, and my eyes locked on Raiden's almond orbs. He licked his lips in a slow and sensual movement that made my mouth dry. My thighs pressed together in remembrance of where his tongue had been just hours before.

Heat rushed across my face and through my chest. I jerked my eyes away from his and found myself staring at a pair of icy cold ones. All the color in my face evaporated as I took in Jack's expression. I didn't need to wonder if he knew something had happened between Raiden and me. The knowledge was all over his face and stance.

Thankfully, my father saved me from having to explain myself. "Now that we are all here, you can be on your way."

I turned my attention away from Jack trying to ignore the guilt in my belly and instead attempted to focus on the road before us. Only there was no carriage. In fact, there was no mode of transport whatsoever. That wasn't right. How did they expect us to get there?

Jack and Raiden didn't seem bothered by the

lack of carriage, but as I turned to them, I realized why. They shifted their stance, and their backs began to shimmer.

Damn him. I shot a glare at my father but got distracted by the sight of Jack's and Raiden's wings appearing.

Thin and long, Jack's wings were the color of freshly fallen snow and scattered with snowflakes. My fingers ached to touch them. I took an unconscious step toward him, one hand reaching toward his wings as a desperate need filled me.

I stopped, taking a deep breath and shutting my eyes as I turned away to get ahold of myself. Only when I opened them, it was almost worse.

Raiden's wings crackled and shifted like lightning, making them seem both unpredictable and dangerous at the same time.

They were nearly the most magnificent things I'd ever seen, rivaled only by Jack's. As my gaze flitted between the pair of them, I tried not to cry.

"What is it?" Raiden asked as he and Jack turned to me. "Have you changed your mind?"

"No," I half laughed and looked down briefly, embarrassed at the whole situation. "It's not that."

"Then please spit it out so we can be on our

way," Jack snapped, affirming once more what I already knew. He was pissed.

Locking eyes with Jack, I focused on my rage. If I didn't, I'd never get through this. "My father seems to have forgotten an important detail about our trip. One that I'm afraid will cause our journey to be a bit more complicated."

Everyone's attention went to my father who had the audacity to look surprised. "I apologize, Maya, I thought you were over your little fear of heights. Apparently, I was wrong." He huffed.

"You're afraid of heights?" Raiden questioned me with an astonished expression. I knew exactly what he was thinking. How could a dragon be afraid of heights? But it wasn't heights I was afraid of, though, it was what everyone had settled on being the reason behind my lack of wings.

Crossing my arms over my chest, I scowled. "It's not that. I don't have my wings yet."

The group quieted, and I didn't dare look at their faces. My sister and mother probably were trying not to look at me with pity. My father no doubt was gloating at having made me look the fool. Jack and Raiden were probably trying to find some excuse to get out of this whole thing because who really wanted to mate with a dragon who couldn't fly.

"Am I understanding this correctly?" Jack asked all the coolness in his voice gone. "You are well over the normal age, and you have not achieved your wings?"

"No, I haven't," I snapped, my eyes flickering up to his briefly before looking away, the understanding in them was too much for me to handle. "They never came in no matter how hard I tried. I trained and trained until I was the fastest and strongest of my class but still… nothing." I didn't bother to hide the bitterness in my voice.

When no one said anything, I knew it was over. They would leave which in hindsight was what I wanted, right? I could go back to Earth and father could find someone else to be his heir.

My eyes burned with angry tears. The Western Lord was cruel when he wanted to be, and it seemed like I had royally pissed him off. I turned away from the group not wanting them to see me cry, but a hand stopped me from walking away.

Glancing down at my shoulder, I was surprised to find the large, pale hand of Jack. My gaze followed up his arm and until they settled on a pair of eyes full of understanding and patience. A stray tear leaked out of my eyes, and I tried to turn away before they could turn to disgust, but Jack wouldn't let me.

His hand cupped the side of my face, his palm cool against my hot skin. Jack stroked his thumb across my face, wiping away my tears, and for the first time since we had met, he smiled. If I'd thought he was handsome before, it didn't hold a candle to now. When he smiled, his face had a truly ethereal quality. One that made me feel almost unworthy to be in his presence.

"We are not as different as you might think," he took a deep, bracing breath, "I, too, did not receive my wings until well after my peers."

"What did you do?" The question came out small and wavering.

"Nothing actually," he replied simply causing my face to fall. "Because I found out the only thing stopping them was me. I was so worried about not gaining my wings, so afraid of bringing dishonor to my family, I couldn't reach that next peak of power."

"So, you're saying I'm the reason I can't fly?" I cocked a brow, feeling even more confused and hopeless than before.

"Yes." He nodded, offering me another blinding

smile. "Once you find what is stopping you, you will find your wings." Jack leaned forward as if to tell me a secret. "And trust me, those who take the longest to blossom are the ones who shine the brightest."

My eyes went to his intricate wings. They were spectacular, and if that was what I had to look forward to, I could probably wait a bit longer to get mine.

"Well, that's all good and well, but that does not help us now," my father growled in distaste. "We'll have to call a carriage which will add two days to the trip. Putting us off schedule."

I could have beaten my father just then. The moment he opened his mouth and started spouting out his negative crap, Jack dropped his hand from my face and stepped away. His back straightened and the beautiful smile on his face smoothed into his usual pensive expression.

I opened my mouth to say something but stopped myself. We'd had a moment there, but it was gone. I didn't know him well enough to call him out on the mask he was determined to keep up. If it had been Ryan or Bianca, I'd tell them to cut the crap, but with dragons, pride played a big part in our personalities. If I pointed it out in front of everyone, he'd never forgive me.

Isn't that what you want? A part of me asked. To make them not want you so you can go home?

I thought I did, but the more I got to know these men, the more I wanted to find out more. I'd just have to play by the rules until I could figure out what it was I really wanted and hopefully with my heart fully in one piece.

7

Raiden and Jack both offered to carry me to the Southern Region, but I promptly refused not wanting to be humiliated even further. While they had both been lovely in regards to my lack of wings, I was still sensitive about it. Though, had I known the carriage ride would be this awkward, I might have sucked it up.

"Are you comfortable, Maya?" Jack asked in the seat next to Raiden.

"I'm fine," I muttered for the millionth time since we had headed out.

They had both agreed I should have one side all to myself while they shared the other. I didn't have the heart to argue but seeing the two large men squished next to each other almost made me feel bad. Almost.

"It will be dark soon," Raiden commented, his eyes out the window. Raiden hadn't said much since we'd left, his attention on the passing scenery the whole time. I wasn't sure what this change of mood meant, but whatever the reason, I couldn't find the energy to care.

"We should find somewhere to camp for the night," Jack replied, waving a hand outside of the window to signal the driver. "I smell water up ahead, be prepared to stop." He hollered out to the driver and then turned his attention to me. "Would this be all right with you?"

The fact that he even bothered to ask me earned him brownie points. If it had been my father or really most males in his position, they wouldn't have bothered to see what I wanted to do. Too full of themselves to think their decision might not be the right one. It was good to know Jack had a good head on his shoulders.

"I'm sure that's fine," I muttered, glancing out the window. The forest covering most of the western lands had thinned out over the course of our journey, revealing the large mountains surrounding the Southern region. As I inhaled, the faint scent of mineral-filled water touched my senses. What do you know, Jack was right. There was water.

The carriage jerked to a halt, throwing me from my seat and into Raiden's lap. Clutching his shirt, I peeked up at him sheepishly. "Uh, sorry about that."

Placing his hands on my shoulders, Raiden's lips curled up in the first grin since the journey had started, "Haven't I told you before, you can fall onto me anytime?"

As I tried to scramble from Raiden's lap, Jack snorted and leapt out of the carriage. I moved to follow, but before I could get far, Raiden grabbed my waist and lifted me into his lap. Eyes wide, my hands automatically went to his chest to push him off.

"What are you doing?" I sharply whispered, my eyes searching out the carriage window for Jack and the driver. Unfortunately, while the driver seemed oblivious to what we were doing, Jack seemed to be rather pointedly ignoring us.

Raiden's hand settled on my inner thigh, jerking my attention back to him with a gasp. "I'm reminding you of what I can give you."

Licking my lips, I gathered my strength and

pushed his hand away before jumping out of his lap. "Believe me," I gave him a sharp look, "I haven't forgotten, but this isn't the right time or place for a refresher."

Climbing out of the carriage before he could reply, I hurried over to where Jack and the driver were discussing where to set up the tents.

"Nice of you to join us," Jack said, barely glancing at me before fixing his eyes on Raiden. "Do you have any preference on where we put the tents?"

"Um... not really," I said, swallowing hard as Jack turned his attention back to me. I could feel Raiden's gaze on my back, and though part of me wanted to look back at him, I resisted.

"What about you?" Jack asked as Raiden sidled over.

"Oh, you know me. Always up for anything." Raiden's hand gently caressed my bare arm as he turned to look at Jack.

"Well, that's helpful." Jack snorted before turning to the driver. "I guess we'll just leave them here." He nodded to Raiden and me. "Can you two set the pegs for this one while we lay out the others?"

"Okay," I said, glad he included me. Normally, male dragons would have told me to wait idly by.

"Your wish is my command," Raiden said, a silly grin flashing across his face as Jack and the driver moved off to unroll the next tent.

Ignoring them, I grabbed a handful of pegs and a hammer before heading to the corner. Only, when I bent over to set the pegs, Raiden pressed his front against my backside.

"Here let me get that," he said as he ground his hardness between the crease of my pants.

A tiny yelp of surprise escaped me, and as the hammer slipped from my grip, my hand shot out to keep me from falling face first onto the ground. Only instead of catching myself in time, Raiden caught me. His strong arm wrapped around my waist, easily holding me steady.

"Not cool," I snapped, wriggling out of Raiden's grip as I straightened. "I'm going to find some firewood." I shoved the pegs in my other hand against his bare chest. "You can finish here."

I practically ran away from the campsite before he could stop me. My feet kept moving until I was well into the woods. I glanced around, and when I didn't see any of them, I fell against the base of a tree with a heavy sigh. These men would be the death of me. At this rate, I didn't see any scenario where I didn't end up with my legs behind my ears before the trip was over. Which I supposed was the whole point of the quest.

"I thought you were getting firewood?" Raiden's voice pulled me out of my thoughts. He stood above me, one hand on the tree trunk as he smirked down at me. His positioning put me right at the line of his pants, and the evidence of his arousal was still going strong.

Swallowing thickly, I turned so I could backpedal away from him and his tempting scent. "I was just taking a break."

"But you haven't even started yet," he teased, following after me like a wolf would stalk his prey.

"Weren't you supposed to help with the tents?" I found my feet and started toward the sound of water, not really thinking about finding firewood anymore.

"Perhaps, but what would your father think if something were to happen to you? No, I thought it best if I help you." With every step I took, Raiden was right there behind me, not quite next to me but trailing a bit behind as if worried I'd take off at any moment. Which to be honest, I wanted to.

"Fine." I broke the clearing of the woods and

saw a waterfall pouring into a large pond. Water, yes, I needed something to cool down this heat I couldn't get rid of.

As Raiden left the forest, he said something I didn't catch.

"What?" I turned back toward him right as my foot slid in a patch of mud. My feet went out from under me, and I landed flat on my back. Breath rushed from my lungs as I lay there dazed.

"Are you okay?" Raiden rushing over to me.

"I'm fine, just… look I don't need to explain myself!" I snapped, waving him off as I got to my feet.

"Oh, I understand." Raiden laughed. "If you wanted a spa day, we could have stopped at the temples on the way. All you had to do was ask."

Wrinkling my nose in disgust, I swept my leg out and hit him with the same trick I had used on Ned. Raiden hit the ground with a splat causing the muddy water to splash up around us. I didn't have a chance to celebrate my victory before he leapt on top of me.

"So, that's how it is going to be?" He chuckled, wrapping one arm around my waist and pulling me down into the mud with him. The mud slid into my clothing making everything squishy and cold. I fought against him, trying to get away from the gross feeling, but then he rolled us over and over in the mud until we were both covered from head to toe. By the end, I was giggling and snorting along with him, and all my worry and stress from before was gone.

Raiden inched up to his feet and offered me a hand. I gladly accepted but almost lost my balance again forcing me to hold onto his waist for support.

Smiling down at me, he rubbed a muddy hand across my face as he pushed my hair back. "There she is."

I frowned at his statement but didn't have time to respond before he picked me up and tossed me in the pond.

"What the hell was that for?" I sputtered, fixing him with a glare.

"You were frowning." He shrugged.

"So you thought I needed to be wet too?" I growled, slapping the water.

"No, I thought you needed to have fun and stop worrying so much," Raiden said as he began to tread into the water. "Didn't Jack tell you before? You just need to relax."

I crossed my arms over my chest and leveled

him with a stare. "And you just decided you would be the one to help me?"

"Pretty much." He looked around. "After all, I don't see anyone else around."

He was waist deep in the water by the time he reached me, and as I looked him up and down, I snorted.

"What makes you think you'll be able to make me relax?" I asked, gesturing at his mud-covered chest. "You don't know anything about me."

"What makes you think I can't?" He cocked a brow and gave me a salacious grin, "I believe I did pretty well this morning."

Even though I was in cold water, my whole body lit up at the memory. My mouth opened and closed like a gaping fish, and for a moment, I was completely at a loss for words. I knew what my body's opinion was. It thought Raiden was more than equipped to help me relax and definitely wanted his assistance again. My head though told me this was a bad idea. A very bad one that would only lead to more heartache later.

"Don't you?" Raiden asked, causing the water around us to slosh as he came toward me. I placed my wet hand on his bare chest where his shirt was plastered against his pectorals. The water from my palms trailed down through the mud, revealing his tanned skin beneath.

"Don't I what?" I asked a bit distracted by our closeness, and as his hands found my waist and slipped beneath the hem of my shirt, my mind became overridden by the urgent needs of my body.

Instead of asking again, Raiden bent down and captured my lips with his. One hand came up behind my neck, angling me so he could take full advantage of my mouth. My nipples hard already from the water temperature brushed against his chest, and a wave of pleasure caused my knees to buckle. Raiden wrapped an arm around my waist, keeping me from going under as he pulled me closer.

As Raiden broke our kiss, he lifted me from the water and sat me on a rock protruding out just before the waterfall. The water sprayed onto completely drenching us and removing the remainder of the mud from Raiden. I had to admit he looked even better wet than he did dry, and as my eyes raked down his body, I couldn't help but wonder if it would be even better without his clothes.

My hand already ahead of my thoughts, pulled

at the buttons of his shirt until they popped open exposing his abs and chest to me. I pulled my mouth away from his so I could fully appreciate what my hands were feeling.

"Wow." The word came out of my mouth before I could stop it, causing Raiden to chuckle.

His hands touched the edge of my shirt, sliding it up along my stomach but stopping beneath my breasts. Raiden seemed to be waiting for my permission which was a complete one-sixty from the way he had commanded me in the bedroom. I couldn't figure out which one I liked better.

Instead, of answering, I lifted my arms allowing him to pull my shirt up and over my head leaving me only in my bra. This time he didn't ask as his hand unsnapped the clip in the back and pulled the straps down my arms. The water touched my breasts, causing me to hiss at the cold.

"Are you cold?" he asked, grabbing me by my butt and pinning me between him and the rock. "Let me warm you up."

My hands buried themselves in the strands of his hair as his hot mouth covered the tip of my breast. I wrapped my legs around his waist and rocked against him. Raiden switched between my breasts before releasing it with a drag of his teeth.

The combination of pleasure and pain caused my hips to buck and my patience to wear thin.

"Now," I gasped, pulling at the waistband of his pants, not even thinking that I still hadn't removed mine. Raiden had though. He unwrapped my legs from around him and pushed my pants down my hips. They were soaked through and getting them down was a struggle. I would have been irritated by how long it took to remove them, but the moment they were off, Raiden was stroking and teasing me.

One arm hoisted me back up while the other drove me into insanity. The press of him against me almost caused me to cry out my release already, but Raiden wasn't done with me yet. Just as I was about to find my peak, he slid into me with one smooth motion.

A choking sound ripped from my throat, and I had a hard time catching my breath. The fullness of finally being joined together was better than I had ever imagined. My inner dragon growled her approval and urged me on.

Not one to deny her, I threw my head back against the rock and let him have me. Raiden pressed his mouth to my collarbone as we moved together, the water splashing against us with each thrust of his hips.

Unlike this morning, there was no teasing, no demanding except for the force of him inside of me. My cries of pleasure echoed off the surrounding rocks, and for a moment, I feared someone would hear us. But the thought disappeared when Raiden slipped a hand between us to help me over the edge.

My nails dug into his shoulders as I screamed out. Raiden kept going, driving me further and further into oblivion. When he finally grunted out his own release, I was so far gone I didn't think my legs would even hold me.

Breathing heavily, I held onto him for fear of drowning if I stood on my own. Our eyes locked for a moment, and we both gave a weak laugh.

"So?" he asked, looking down at my naked body. "Are you relaxed yet?"

I didn't know if it was the floating sensation in my head I was feeling or Raiden himself, but his question caused a playful side of me to emerge. Instead of telling him I was quite relaxed, I shifted my hips to rock against him, making him hiss.

"Not quite yet."

8

Dark had started to fall by the time Raiden and I found our way back to the camp. When we stepped out of the wood clearing and into the camp Jack and our driver had set up, I realized too late I had forgotten to get wood, well, at least the kind I was supposed to get, anyway.

I hoped they wouldn't notice our little mess up, but Jack's narrowed gaze didn't ease my worries. Nor the way his nostrils flared. The water should have covered up what Raiden and I had done but obviously not well enough.

"Why are you all wet?" the accusation in his voice wasn't lost on me as Raiden and I came closer.

Raiden didn't seem to have any issue at all with Jack knowing about us getting together. In fact, he puffed out his chest and wrapped an arm around my shoulders in a possessive manner. Not wanting to give him or Jack the wrong idea, I shrugged it off before moving over to where the driver had already started a fire.

"We fell in the mud." I left it at that though I doubted I would be able to for long. Settling down by the fire, I took my boots and socks off so they could dry. I purposely ignored the way Raiden and Jack stared at each other.

"Your Highness," our driver said, moving by my side and giving me a slight inclination of his head by way of a greeting. "Would you like something to eat?" He offered me a plate with some bread and cheese.

I took it from him with a grateful smile. "Thank you..." I trailed off, his name not coming to mind.

"Herbert." I tried not to make a face, but I seemed to have failed miserably because Herbert laughed his brown eyes twinkling in the firelight. "I know it's not the most dragon-like name out there." When I gave a nervous chuckle, he added, "It could have been worse, I almost ended up named after my great-uncle Mary."

This time I didn't hold back my wince. As Herbert and I shared a laugh the air around my potential mates crackled, and the temperature dropped. Great. Just great.

Exchanging a look with Herbert, I sat my plate down before standing. Eyes narrowed and jaw clenched, I stomped across the camp and stepped between the two of them. Their powers bit at my skin, and I forced back a yelp.

Irritation pricked at me, and I gave them both a hard shove. My attack jolted them enough to break their staring match causing their powers to lessen. Their gazes turned away from each other and focused on me.

"What do you think you two are doing?" Hands on my hips, I glared up at them.

"He started it." Raiden jerked his head at Jack. "I didn't do anything."

"Oh real mature," I snorted. "Why don't you chill out, Raiden?" Gesturing to where Herbert had laid out several more plates. "Maybe get something to eat?"

"Fine." Raiden shot Jack one more warning look before dropping his arms to his sides and heading over to the fire. My eyes trailed after him until he had settled beside our driver before snapping to Jack. He stood there silent as stone.

"So, what's your problem?" I asked trying not to sound more irritated than I already felt. "I'd expect this kind of stuff from Raiden, but I thought you would be above it."

Lips pressed into a thin line, Jack's eyes swirled with a mixture of power and emotion. "So did I."

"Then what is it?" I stepped closer to him, half-wanting to reach out to comfort him but, at the same time, worried I'd be burned from his chilly gaze.

"Did you or did you not mate with that man-child?" The anger in his voice shocked me more so than his question.

I glanced down at the ground, guilt clogging up my throat. Of course, he would find out. Why did I think he wouldn't? Neither Raiden nor I had been very discreet. Suddenly, I remembered how I had screamed out at the waterfall. Had he heard me? Was it more than just scenting it on us? My face heated at the thought, and I couldn't bring myself to meet Jack's gaze.

"As I thought," Jack answered for me. Power radiated from him, freezing me to the bone. "Is there any point of my being here? Should I just leave now since you clearly have chosen your mate?"

"No!" I snapped and then lowered my voice so Raiden and Herbert couldn't hear. "I mean, no, I haven't chosen anyone yet."

"Then why did you mate with *him?*" Clear disdain filled his words, and I couldn't help but want to defend the lightning dragon.

"You have no right to be like this. He has made an effort to get to know me. He has been trying to do what you were brought here to do. While you," I shoved a finger in his hard chest, "all you've done is glower and order people around. It seems more like you are looking for a reason to leave."

Jack didn't say anything for a moment, and I thought maybe I had gone too far. Then he took me by the waist and drew me against him, causing me to gasp in surprise. The coolness of his body combined with the heat of mine caused my nipples to harden and a shiver to run through me. Even more so when his lips covered mine.

Unlike Raiden's kisses, which were demanding and always in control, Jack's were hesitant, unsure as if he didn't know what I liked. Not unpleasant but not enough to get my motor going. Still, there was lots of potential. He just needed some guidance.

Trying to help us both along, I took charge. Sliding my hands into his long tresses, I angled my mouth along his, slipping my tongue out to trace the line of his lips. His hands flexed on my waist before he opened his mouth, allowing me inside.

A throat clearing interrupted our embrace, and both Jack and I came away breathing heavily. Our eyes searched for the one who interrupted us and landed on Herbert, who had a deep blush on his aged cheeks. A bit flustered and embarrassed, I dropped my hands from his hair, letting them settle on his chest. Jack didn't release me but stepped back so we no longer pressed against one another. From the hardness I'd felt, it hadn't been for my benefit but his.

"Well," I started, staring at Jack's chest. "That was different."

"But it didn't make a difference," Jack said bitterness filling his voice as he removed his hands from my waist. Instantly, I missed his touch. Jack had given me a glimpse into what kind of man he really was, and I needed – no wanted – to know more.

"Ugh." I threw my hands down as a grimace

replaced my smile. "Yes, I mated with Raiden, but that doesn't mean I'm pregnant."

"But you could be," Jack's eyes went to my flat stomach. "Then there would be no point in my being here."

I sighed and ran a hand through my hair. Freaking high maintenance men! I could kill the lot of them.

"It's not likely." Raiden came up beside us, surprising me with his words. "We all know how hard it is for our females to get pregnant. The way I see it, no one has won until Maya is pregnant, which might take weeks or even months and lots and lots of fucking." He winked at me, causing my body to heat and my thighs to press together.

"So, what? You want us to share her?" Jack asked. The disbelief in his voice made it clear he didn't think it possible. "How would we know who won then? Either of us could get her pregnant."

"Sure, why not? And we'll find out when the baby is born of course." Raiden shrugged a shoulder and then asked me, "As long as you don't mind, Maya?"

Licking my lips, my eyes darted between the two men. I'd always thought I would be a one-dragon kind of woman, but the thought of these two attractive males sharing me caused arousal to flood my body. I could just see myself being taken by one of them while I pleasured the other with my mouth. The image caused a shudder of desire to shake my form. Jack and Raiden breathed in suddenly, no doubt taking in my scent. I didn't know why, but it embarrassed me for them to know.

Raiden shoved me to the side just as an arrow zipped past. Pain flashed through me as I hit the ground and Herbert cried out in alarm.

Agony filled his face as he grasped the spot where an arrow had punctured his arm. Blood flowed through his fingers as he gripped the spot his arm.

I scrambled across the ground toward him, but before I made it far, Raiden blocked my path. He knelt down beside me, one hand on my shoulder, but instead of looking at me, his intense dark eyes searched the tree line.

"Stay down," he murmured in a voice so low only I'd be able to hear it. As Raiden spoke, lightning began to crackle along his free hand, and as I turned away from the arcing electricity, I saw Jack.

He was on my other side, shielding me from whatever lurked in the tree line. Jack's form began to glow a faint white, energy cascading off him like snowflakes.

"What's there? Do you see some—"

My words were cut off as six dragons with wings of flames burst from the trees. They didn't even glance at Herbert as the poor guy writhed in pain by the fireside but went straight toward Raiden, Jack, and me.

"Stay back," Jack roared, flinging a spray of crystalline energy from his hand that took the two lead dragons in the chest. They stopped moving so suddenly, it was like seeing someone hit with liquid nitrogen. They froze in mid-movement as hoarfrost spread down their bodies, locking them to the ground in ice until they looked like ice sculptures.

Unfortunately, his attack caused the other four to dive sideways, avoiding the blasts. As Jack began to glow once more, Raiden grunted beside me, and I jerked my attention back to him.

Lightning filled both his hands, as he stepped forward, lashing out at the two dragons angling toward us.

As he unleashed a volley at the left one, causing it to leap back a step, the other darted in. His flaming gauntlet lashed out, right as Raiden side-stepped. The blow whooshed over my head, causing a wave of heat to lick the sweat from my body.

A shriek rippled from my lips right before Raiden slammed his open palm into the dragon's chest. Lightning leapt across our attacker's armor moments before he was flung backward in an explosion of sparks.

Unfortunately, that attack left Raiden wide open to the other guy. Scrambling to my feet, I hurried to block a blow headed straight for Raiden's head. Slow from disuse, I drew my magic from within and pulled at the ground beneath us. Vines whipped out of the ground and wrapped around the attacker's body, knocking him off his feet. Only, as he crashed to the ground, his hands lashed out, grabbing onto my shirt and pulling me down with him.

Pain shot through me as I landed hard on my stomach. The breath exploded from my lungs as the man reached out and grabbed hold of my ankle. As he pulled me toward him, I cursed. My vines should have held him back, kept him from moving, but already I could see they'd been charred to ash. That shouldn't have happened so quickly. Were they weak from not using my power while I was banished?

"Don't you know it's not nice to grab a lady?" I

cried, kicking out with my other leg. The heel of my boot smashed into the man's face, shattering his nose in a spray of blood.

His grip slackened for a moment, and as I tried to pull myself free, he shook his head, reorienting himself. Tears spilled from his eyes as his grip tightened and he pulled me back toward him while throwing himself forward with his legs.

He landed hard on my thighs, pinning me with his greater weight as I struggled against him. I might be a dragon, but compared to the mammoth above me, I didn't stand a chance in a fair fight.

I reached down deep, calling on my magic as he crawled on top of me, pinning my arms beneath his knees. I reached out, calling upon the vines once again, and as they burst from the ground, he backhanded me across the face. As the taste of blood filled my mouth, my concentration shattered, and the vines fell lifelessly to the ground.

"Maya," Raiden cried out. "Just hang on!"

Lightning rippled along his body, causing the sky above us to flicker as he flung his attacker off into the brush once more. The man holding me down hesitated a moment, his attention shifting toward Raiden.

Raiden lifted one hand toward the sky, and as

he did, a bolt of lightning exploded from the nearly cloudless sky with a thunder crack that nearly blew out my eardrums. The man holding me cried out in shock as Raiden caught the lightning like he was Zeus himself.

As Raiden reared back, the lightning forked outward into a trident of crackling energy that he flung through the air.

The trident took the man on top of me in the chest, pierced through his chest plate like it was made of tissue paper, and punched out his back with so much force it ripped the man off of me. The moment he hit the ground, the smell of charred flesh hit my nose as electricity pulsed through his entire body, flash frying him in an instant.

"Are you okay?" Raiden asked, holding his hand out to me.

"Thank you!" I cried, gripping his hand and letting him haul me to his feet. Only as he did, the first attacker came charging toward us, a dagger in his hand.

Without missing a beat, Raiden whirled around, snatching up his crackling trident and whipping it outward. The tri-blades punched into our attacker's throat, and as Raiden twisted, tearing out the man's throat, electricity leapt from the weapon. Not that it mattered because he was already dying as the lightning cooked him too.

"Stay near me," Raiden said, putting one arm against me as a sound like shattering crystal filled the air.

I spun to find Jack standing over a bunch of frozen chunks that even all the king's horses and all the king's men wouldn't be putting back together again.

Behind him, the two men from earlier were still frozen.

"Clear," Jack said, meeting Raiden's eyes.

"Almost." Raiden shifted his stance and threw the trident. It hit the pair of men, shattering them into pieces.

"I had them under control," Jack said in a calm voice as the trident returned to Raiden's hand like it had a mind of its own.

"I believe you." Raiden shrugged. "But dead men tell no tales."

Ignoring their banter, my eyes fixed on the trident still crackling in Raiden's hand. "Have you always been able to do that?" I pointed at the weapon.

"No. I haven't." His eyes followed mine, his

brow creasing between his eyes as he stared at it like he'd just noticed it was there. "Only the elite of my kind are able to manifest their powers into weapons. I'd never quite been able to reach that level."

Frowning, I reached out, almost touching it but jerked my hand back when it disappeared. "It's amazing." I swallowed, about to ask more when an agonizing groan reminded me we weren't completely unscathed.

"Herbert!" I ran to the older man's side, looking over the arrow still in his arm. "It doesn't look like it went through the bone."

"Still hurts like hell, though," Herbert grunted and then cried out when I touched the arrow's shaft.

"Sorry." I winced as I tried to figure out how to remove it without causing him any more pain. A presence appeared to my right, and I glanced over to see Jack kneeling at my side. The calm radiating from him instantly lowered my worry.

Without a word, he shoved the arrow further through Herbert's arm until the head was all the way out. As Herbert cried out in pain, he snapped the end and pulled it completely out from the other side.

"Wow, how did you know to do that?" My

mouth dropped open in surprise as Jack pulled out a bundle of bandages.

"All of our soldiers are trained in field medicine. Isn't yours?" The way Jack said it made it sound like it was something everyone should know. Then he set to work on the wound.

"Uh... I don't know." Sadly, I was telling the truth. As the princess, I did get training like all the rest of the dragons in my region, but medical training had never been something I'd been interested in. If there had been training, I'd missed it.

As Herbert continued to whimper, Jack shot me a look. "Do you want me to show you?"

Before I could answer, Raiden moved next to me. "I scouted the area, and didn't see any others, but that doesn't mean there aren't more. I think it would be better if I moved the princess to the carriage while you finish up." He met Jack's eyes. "Just in case there're more of them."

"Okay." Jack looked like he wanted to argue, but instead, he just nodded and turned his attention to Herbert.

"I'm not some delicate flower," I said, as Raiden helped me to my feet.

"I never thought you were," Raiden replied, nodding. "But an arrow from the bushes will kill a princess as well as it will kill a driver." He took a long breath. "This way, Jack and Herbert will be the next targets. It will give me time to get you out of here."

Not wanting to think about that, I decided to follow Raiden. After all, we still had no idea how many more of them there were, and while I didn't like the idea of leaving Jack outside unguarded, he seemed plenty capable of taking care of himself.

"So," I said, glancing at Raiden. "The trident... what do you think gave your powers such a super boost?"

Raiden stroked his chin with his fingertips before giving me a lopsided grin.

"What's that look about?" I asked, confused.

Rocking on his heels, Raiden smirked. "You know."

Still lost I turned to Jack and Herbert, hoping for some insight into what the hell Raiden was talking about. They apparently, weren't so lost. Herbert's face had turned a bit red, but it could have been from the pain and not embarrassment. The tension in Jack's jaw finally clued me in.

"No," I said, shaking my head. "You don't think..." Raiden's grin widened as I realized what they referred to. "Why in the world would you think us...?" I gestured between Raiden and me animatedly.

"Yes. I do." Raiden crossed his arms over his chest with a stern nod.

Speechless, I didn't know what to think. While the thought that having sex with me would be enough to cause some kind of power jolt was flattering, to say the least, it was a little hard to swallow.

"It's not unheard of," Jack said as he finished wrapping Herbert's arm. "There have been cases of mated pairs gaining new or improved powers, though it's rare. Since you are the daughter of a lord, the likelihood you would cause such a reaction would be higher than others."

"So, what?" I gestured wildly. "Does that mean every guy I sleep with will gain some kind of extra power boost?"

Jack moved to the other side of the fire and shrugged. "I wouldn't know but possibly."

I didn't know how I felt about that. Having to mate for an heir was one thing, being a new source of power was another. Unfortunately, Jack didn't seem like he would be helping me figure it out either.

The ice dragon's face closed down, obviously done with the conversation. Maybe because of the subject or maybe because he thought if he showed any interest in gaining new abilities it would make me less attracted to him. Either way, I didn't have time to worry about his feelings, the remains of our attackers still lay around us.

"Who do you think attacked us?" I nodded my head toward one of the dead fire dragons.

Raiden glanced around. "Maybe Lord Amun doesn't want us to come?"

9

We stayed the night where we had gotten attacked because it was too dark to pack back up, though we disposed of the bodies further into the woods. I didn't like the idea, but since it seemed like a scouting party upon closer examination, it seemed unlikely we'd get attacked soon. After all, as far as we knew, none of them had gotten away. Besides, Herbert was too hurt to attempt traveling at night. Instead, we took turns standing guard, even Herbert with his injured arm.

The men still babied me, which I found irritating though I partially found myself thankful for it. I had five years of pretending to be human, it seemed I did too good of a job. I shouldn't have had such a problem with my magic against the fire dragon. Uprooting vines and trees used to be second nature to me. Of course, I hadn't used it while on Earth, there wasn't any need for it. I hoped it wasn't a case of use it or lose it. Now that I actually had cause to fight, I couldn't let myself hang back in the shadows while the men fought my battles.

"Can't sleep?" Raiden sat next to where I lay on my mat.

Shifting to my elbow, I met his gaze. "Not really. Hard to sleep with all that's going on. Though, my body really hates me for it."

"I understand." He laced his fingers together over his knees, his eyes moving to the tree line. "I think we all are a little bit on edge now."

"Do you think we'll encounter more attacks?"

Raiden shook his head. "There's no telling. I hope not. But we are still half a day away from Lord Amun's palace. We can't let our guard down."

We sat in silence for a moment. The silence had an intimate feel to it, and I couldn't deal with that right now. I smirked and shoved Raiden on the leg. "We'll be safe as long as we have you and your new powers." I shook my head and smiled. "I think the bad guys will think twice before attacking again."

Raiden returned my grin, obviously proud of his performance. "It's because of you, though. If it hadn't been for you, I wouldn't have these powers and then where would we be?"

The truth in his assessment made my face drop. I didn't like the idea of being someone's hero. Like all of our lives depended on me and my magic touch. Hero's didn't live long, and I planned on living to a ripe old age.

"Anyway," Raiden continued. "It's going to be morning soon. You should get some rest." He nodded toward my bed mat.

I lay back down and tried to go back to sleep, but my mind whirled with all that had happened. By the time I fell asleep the sky had begun to lighten and too soon Raiden shook me awake, and we were off again.

The trip still had a tense feel to it, but this time it was for a different reason. Everyone's eyes stayed on the tree line and the sky anticipating an attack at any moment. It wasn't until we saw the gates of the Southern Mountain kingdom that any of us began to relax.

"Finally," I sighed, sitting back in my seat.

Raiden's leg bumped against mine as he said, "Don't relax just yet. We aren't in the city yet."

I opened my mouth to argue, but Jack interrupted, "He's right. We should not let our guard down now nor when we get inside. For all we know, Lord Amun ordered the attack."

Frowning, I leaned out the window slightly to look at the gates. Tall walls made out of tan stone, they didn't seem too welcoming. Even when we were let through the steel doors, there were no guards to greet us. Instead, they stood at attention along the top of the wall and just inside of the gate doors.

"Cheerful place isn't it?" I muttered, but neither of my companions responded, their attention focused on the passing city.

The buildings we drove by were made out of the same kind of stone as the wall, but unlike my own kingdom, the shutters were closed. The doors tightly shut. The stalls of what could have been the marketplace were covered but not empty. Like they were just on a break and would be back later.

"Think they were expecting us?" Raiden suggested. His eyes taking in the hurried attempt to close their stalls.

"Hmm." Jack rubbed his chin. "I think they were expecting an attack."

"What makes you say that?" My brows furrowed, trying to figure out where he came to that conclusion.

"I've seen this kind of reaction to visitors before in some of the small towns along the coast," Jack explained. "They are so used to being raided, they don't bother to hide their valuables but seek to protect their families first, hoping the attackers will take the easily accessible goods and leave."

"And the guys who attacked us in the woods?" I left the question open in the air.

"They were probably some of the same ones who have been attacking them." Jack nodded to the blatantly left out golden box and gems. Anyone could have come by and taken them without repercussions. It made me feel better about our trip, but worse at the same time.

We continued on the path, seeing more of the same until we reached the palace. The carriage came to a stop before the gates, and Herbert dropped down before coming around and opening my door. Before I could get out, Jack held his hand up signaling to me to let him go first. I glanced to

Raiden who nodded his agreement. Reluctantly, I settled back into my seat.

After a moment, Jack's hand popped back into the window as he waved us out. I inched out of the carriage with Raiden closely behind me. Jack stood at my front wedging me between him and Raiden as we made our way to the front doors. A man and woman came out to greet us, the first friendly faces we had seen since we arrived.

"Greetings." The woman with dark brown hair and an arrogant stride stopped before us. Her eyes darted to Raiden and then to Jack, lingering on him a little longer than I would have liked before finally landing on me. "You must be Maya." She didn't offer me her hand and seemed genuinely irritated at my presence in general.

"Yes, and you are?" I glanced from her to the man who had stayed a few steps behind her. Hands folded behind his back, he smiled, but it didn't reach his charcoal-colored eyes. Those eyes trailed up and down my form, and I forced back a shudder of disgust.

"I am Lord Amun's advisor, Mon Liz." She turned away from us and headed back toward the doors.

Exchanging a look with my companions, they

seemed as confused as me. Shrugging, I followed after Mon Liz. Her male friend waited until we had passed before trailing after us. I didn't like having him at our backs. We still didn't know if the attack came from the inside or if it had come from whoever had the locals frightened.

"This is odd," Jack commented from my side. The inside of the palace wasn't any cheerier than the outside. The servants were scarce — if they had any at all — and the walls were barren of any of the usual decorative tapestries. Lords loved to flaunt their wealth, but if I didn't know any better, I'd say Lord Amun was only a lord in name alone.

I didn't like how quiet it was nor how Mon Liz had turned her back on us so easily. As if we weren't a threat to any of them. Of course, that wasn't what we came for but still — insulting.

Mon Liz stopped at a pair of double doors and turned to us, not surprised at all that we had followed her. She waited until we settled a few feet away from her before she spoke again.

"I want you to know, I advised against Lord Amun meeting with you." Not like she had been hiding how much disdain she had for us, well not Jack.

"Is that so?" I mused, proud I'd hid the annoyance in my voice. It wouldn't do to anger the very people we were supposed to be creating an alliance with.

"Yes." Her eyes settled on me, narrowing into slits. "I don't think it is wise to meet with foreign dignitaries at a time like this and *any* adviser would tell him the same."

"At a time like this?" Jack asked, taking a step closer to the woman. He offered her a small smile. I would have labeled it as flirtatious had I ever seen it pointed my way. Jealousy billowed in my stomach, surprising me.

Sure, Jack wasn't mine, but he was supposed to be there to win my affections, not flirt with some old bat. His smile had an interesting effect on Mon Liz though. She fluttered her lashes, and her hand came up to her chest as if to still her racing heart.

Twisting her hair between her fingers like a goddamned school girl, she murmured in what I could only call a bedroom voice, "We've been under attack."

"We assumed that much," Raiden snapped. He didn't seem to care for Jack's flirting either, or maybe it was my reaction he didn't like? "Why don't you tell us something we don't know?"

Mon Liz glared at Raiden, but Jack's hand on her shoulder caused it to soften.

"You were saying, my lady?" He brought her hand up to his lips, pressing his mouth to the sagging skin there.

The old bat actually blushed! But it had the desired effect, and she started talking again. "Why from the rogue bandits, of course. They've been badgering us for months now with no relief." She glanced at Raiden and me with a shake of her head. "I told Lord Amun we needed to take care of the problem before you came, or it would make our region seem weak."

Mon Liz was the one who was weak. One pretty face and she sang like a canary, spouting out all kinds of secrets I was sure her lord did not want us to know about.

"Well," Jack said, taking her arm in the crook of his. "Why don't you bring us to your lord, and we can discuss what we can do to help with his bandit problem."

Letting Jack lead her, Mon Liz opened the double doors and gestured us into a large round room. I could only assume it was the throne room though it had no throne. What it did have was a table with a map spread across it. A man stood with his back to us, his face toward the balcony window. When we approached, he didn't even bother to turn around.

"My lord, the Western dignitaries have arrived," Mon Liz announced us.

"Is there a reason you are hanging all over one of the princess's men?" Lord Amun didn't turn as he questioned his adviser. There must have been something in his voice though because Mon Liz dropped her arm from Jack's and took several steps away from him.

I forced myself not to smile at the dejected look on her face. Instead, I stepped toward Jack, taking Mon Liz's place at his side and addressed Lord Amun, "Thank you for having us, Lord Amun. My father will be happy to know you are doing well."

Lord Amun snorted. "I'm assuming my adviser has filled you in on our situation, so you can stop pretending we aren't in distress."

I glanced at Jack before clearing my throat. "Yes, she told us a bit about it."

"We were attacked on our way here," Raiden jumped in, coming up beside me. "Any ideas about that?"

"They were ours?" Lord Amun asked finally turning from the window. Lord Amun, a tall man with a dark red beard and bright blue eyes, could be called a handsome man had it not been for the deforming scar down the side of his face. It seemed like he wasn't the only one who had suffered from the last war.

"Fire dragons?" Raiden asked and then when he nodded said, "Yes. We were attacked by six of them, each wearing a tan uniform. It seemed to be aimed directly for Maya."

Lord Amun stroked the beard on his chin, the half that grew in anyways. "So, they know you are here."

"Who are they?" I asked tired of the whole big mystery. I was ready to know who had tried to kill me and why.

Instead of answering my question, Lord Amun said, "Here is what is going to happen. I will sign your father's treaty, and you will fix our little problem we are having."

I forced back an aggravated sigh. Everyone wanted something for me, but no one wanted to give me anything in return. Or at least, anything I wanted. "I can't agree to that until I know what your problem is."

Lord Amun locked eyes with me and intensity in them that told me the situation was a lot more dire than he made it out to be. "The bandits are the problem. You get rid of them, and I will sign the treaty."

I glanced at Raiden and Jack before holding up a finger to the lord. When he nodded, I drew my companions to the side, worry starting to rise in my throat until it was nearly choking me.

"What should we do?" I said, trying to sound more confident than I felt. This was not a situation I was used to handling. Sure, I could maybe talk down a meeting full of angry programmers, but this? This was way beyond my pay grade.

Jack and Raiden exchanged a look I couldn't read. The look did nothing to quell my anxiousness. We were in over our heads. There were only three of us, four if you counted Herbert, but he wasn't a soldier, and he was injured. That left three people against God only knew how many in this bandit gang.

"I think we should accept," Jack stated after a moment.

Raiden nodded his agreement. "I do too."

"What?" I gasped, not believing what they were saying. "We can't promise to beat some people we don't know. For all we know, we could die before ever getting back to get the treaty signed."

"The men in the woods were not very skilled," Raiden pointed out. "Plus, like you said before, I have my trident."

"That doesn't mean you are unstoppable," I hissed under my breath, knowing the lord watched us from his spot by the window.

"Then why don't you just have sex with ice boy here and give him a power boost too?" Raiden clapped Jack on the shoulder. "Even if it doesn't work, I'm sure it'll take the edge off."

Jack shoved Raiden's hand off of him with a glare.

"I'm not sleeping with Jack!" I couldn't help the rise in my voice. Unfortunately, my words caused Jack to frown. "Not that I don't want to, but I'm not about to screw everyone I know just so we have more power. Being with both of you was already pushing it." I understood how having sex with Jack would make us stronger, but it wasn't like it had been with Raiden. He and I had an instant connection that Jack and I just didn't have. Sure, we were finding our chemistry, but it was far from being enough to hit the sack.

"I agree with the princess," Jack said, an edge in his voice. "I don't want her to sleep with me just to give me power." He shook his head.

"You're just afraid it won't work," Raiden said, voice low. "But you should still try."

"Don't I get a say in this?" I asked, glaring at Raiden. I wasn't some brood mare no matter how much my father thought so.

"Sure, but I don't know what else to tell you, Princess." Raiden crossed his arms over his chest. "That's what I propose."

"And you think we can beat them? Without knowing what we are actually up against?" I asked Jack who I had labeled as the more reasonable of the two. "I mean, the bandits seem to have driven this place into the ground."

"We'll be smart about it. We aren't just going to rush in there without a plan." Raiden answered for him, and they shared another look. Those were really starting to irritate me.

Fingers curled into fists until they bit into my palms, I fought against the urge to stomp my foot. My father must have known about Lord Amun's problem and knew we would have to fix it for him. While I wasn't sure if he'd told the men about it beforehand, I still felt betrayed and ganged up on. Worse, Raiden sort of had a point. It did make sense, given our situation, to sleep with Jack and see if he too got a power boost.

Spinning on my heel, I stomped back over to where Lord Amun waited. "Who's the bastard leader of this group and where can we find him?"

"They have a hideout up to the north in between two sleeping volcanos." Lord Amun folded his hands over in front of him. "The bastard leader, is my son, Firestar."

10

Chest heaving, I felt like the walls were closing in on me. I had to have heard him wrong. That had to be. There was no way Firestar would be here and be the leader of the bandits no less.

Muffled voices tried to talk to me, but I couldn't hear them above the pounding of my pulse in my ears. If it were true, not only would I see Firestar again, but I would have to see him with them. How would I explain that? Any of this?

Just say it was your father's idea a part of me sneered.

While I agreed it hadn't been my idea in the first place. I didn't think Firestar would agree so much. Though, this was assuming he even cared about me anymore. We hadn't seen each other in years, he could have found a mate by now and have a nest of little ones.

A nagging feeling told me it wasn't so. He still thought of me as I did of him. Firestar had impacted my life in the short time we had been together more than anyone I'd ever met. Just thinking of him now caused my heart to race and my hands to sweat. The dragon inside of me made a low growl, she wanted to see him again too.

Someone grabbed me by the arm, and my low growl turned into a fierce one as I turned on them, teeth bared. Raiden's eyes widened, and he released me, putting his hands up in defense. When I realized who it was, I forced back my beast and took a deep breath.

After a moment, I shook my head, giving Raiden an apologetic smile.

"What was that?" Raiden asked still keeping a cautious distance from me.

I didn't know how much I should tell them. Raiden probably wouldn't think anything of it. Of the two men my father had chosen for me, he seemed the more understanding. Jack, on the other hand, had already shown he had a hard time sharing. We hadn't even decided if we could all get along together with just the three of us. We had been attacked before I could even get my answer out.

No, I couldn't tell them about Firestar and me. It would cause more issues than we needed right now. Besides, there was no telling if Firestar would even remember me, right?

"Nothing," I finally said, shaking my head again. "I'm just really pumped to get this over with."

Raiden and Jack didn't look convinced. A slight glance to Mon Liz and I knew she definitely didn't believe me, though I hardly cared what she thought, anyway. Lord Amun had a knowing kind of smile on his face, which made me even more nervous about his request.

Did he know about Firestar and me? I thought only my father had? It wouldn't bode well for this trip if it was all some kind of dubious plot the lord had concocted. But to what end? What was he planning?

I didn't have time to think more on it because my dragons were staring me down as if waiting for me to break. Ignoring their questioning gazes, I kept my eyes on Lord Amun.

"We accept your terms and will leave immediately." I nodded and headed for the door.

The lord's voice stopped me. "There is no hurry." He waved a hand dismissively when I turned to look at him. "You should stay the night refresh yourselves. Volcano ridge is quite far from here." He gestured at Mon Liz, who hopped to attention. "Please make sure they have rooms prepared and dinner is provided."

Lord Amun then turned his back on us, his attention once more out the window. Mon Liz came over to us, this time not sparing a glance toward Jack.

"It looks like we've been dismissed," Jack muttered, placing a hand on the back of my waist. "What would you like to do, Maya?"

I opened my mouth to answer, but Mon Liz interrupted.

"Oh, you must stay!" Her eyes lit up with excitement. "Now that word has gone around the city there will be plenty of things to see, and you won't want to miss them." Her lips curled into a creepy smile. "When do you think you'll have a chance to visit us again?"

I tried again to say we weren't staying, but the interest in Raiden's expression made me pause.

Even Jack looked like he really wanted to see what Mon Liz was on about. Sighing reluctantly, I said, "Very well. It couldn't hurt to stay one night."

Raiden whooped, and I knew I made the right decision. There had been enough seriousness on this trip we needed a bit of fun and touring the city might just be it.

"Has Firestar and his men attacked the palace already?" I asked as Mon Liz escorted us to another part of the palace. Its walls were as barren as the rest of the palace, and I couldn't help but ask what had been on my mind since we arrived.

Mon Liz frowned, glancing at the bare walls. "No, Lord Amun requested all valuables be put in the safe for safekeeping until the raids are dealt with, anyway."

I nodded in understanding. It still baffled me that Firestar had become a lowly bandit. He had been so formidable. Such an honored dragon warrior. What had caused him to revolt against his father of all people?

Mon Liz stopped before a set of double doors and turned to the group. "This is one of the larger rooms. It's always prepared in case of unannounced visitors. You can use it for now until we find something more suitable."

"I'm sure it will be fine." Jack offered her a small smile, causing the old woman to flush.

"As you wish." As Mon Liz moved to leave, neither Jack nor Raiden bothered to ask the more important question.

"Wait." Mon Liz paused at my voice, turning back to me with a raised brow. "Are you telling me this room is for all of us?" I circled my little trio with my hand.

Mon Liz's lips turned down into a confused frown. "I apologize. Lord Amun said these were your men, so I just assumed…"

"No, no. It's fine." I interrupted her as I felt my face heat. "It'll be fine. Right guys?" I glanced at Raiden and Jack for confirmation.

Raiden gave me a thumbs up and a wink, but Jack looked like he had swallowed something foul. Still, he gave a nod of consent. Better than nothing I guess.

"Very well," Mon Liz stated and opened her hands in front of her. "Is there anything else? Or…"

"No." I jumped in and grabbed for the doorknob. "We're good. Thank you for your hospitality."

Darting into the room, I didn't wait for the men to follow me as I made my way to the bathroom. I scanned the room as the door shut behind me. It had all the necessities. A toilet, sink, and a shower. A bathtub large enough to fit all of us caught my eye. I swallowed and tried not to focus on the prospects.

The thought of the two dragons in the other room sharing me was too much for me to handle right now. Not with the possibility that I would see Firestar in less than forty-eight hours. The knowledge both excited and frightened me.

I turned the water at the sink on, splashing my face with the cool liquid. It did little to calm my nerves, nor was it loud enough to block out the sound of Raiden and Jack talking in low voices in the other room. They would no doubt want to interrogate me when I came out.

All the more reason to stay where I was. The coward part of me whispered. Or better yet, climb out the window.

My eyes darted to the small window above the toilet. Small but still large enough I could wiggle through if I needed to. The drop couldn't be that far. We didn't go up any stairs. I could finally get away. Maybe someone in town could make a portal and then I could go back to Earth. Live out my life there and forget about all this.

A silly unachievable fantasy. As much as I wanted to run away and back to my easy Earth life, I couldn't. Not without seeing Firestar. The thought of hurting Raiden and Jack also came to mind, and I found that I didn't want to do that either. Hell, even if I did escape, my father would never allow it. He'd have Ned hunt me down again.

As if knowing my thoughts, there was a soft knock on the door, and Jack's voice followed. "Maya, are you all right?"

"I'm fine," I called out, my voice a bit too hysterical for my liking. "I just need a minute."

"Are you sure?" The concern in Jack's voice made me feel guilty for my earlier thoughts. These guys had dropped everything to be here. Leaving them stranded in another country wouldn't just be wrong, it'd be downright mean.

I sighed and rubbed a hand over my face before going to the door. Turning the knob, I offered Jack a weak smile. "I'm sure. Just a bit overwhelmed."

Jack visibly relaxed at my words. "We don't have to tour the city. We can just rest if that is what you wish? I'm sure Lord Amun will understand."

"No, I want to go. Like Mon Liz said, 'When do

you think you'll have a chance to visit us again?'" I tried to mimic her ridiculous accent, causing Jack to give me a rare smile. "You should do that more, you know."

"What?" Jack asked, moving aside so I could reenter the bedroom.

"Smile more," I murmured a bit distracted by the room before me. Larger than my room back home, the bed had a high canopy of dark redwood, and the mattress could have bedded six people. My face heated at the implications.

"It's great isn't it?" Raiden gave me a knowing grin as he smoothed his hand over the top of the comforter. He leaned back on his elbows, propping one leg up on the end of the bed. Memories of the last time Raiden and I had been in a bed together caused my body to warm.

I couldn't help the smile that came to my face or the slickness between my thighs. The memory was promptly squashed by the sound of disgust behind me.

Twisting around, I stared back at Jack. The coolness in his eyes had returned and that peek I'd had into his shell was gone.

"What's wrong now?" I sighed.

"Seems like the only time I can get your attention is when someone else is interested in me." Jack flipped his long silvery white hair over his shoulder in a way that would have made a pop diva proud.

My eyes shot to Raiden for help, but he simply shrugged. Seemed like I was on my own.

"Yes, it bothered me to see you flirting with Mon Liz," I admitted. Not that it bothered me to say so.

Jack sniffed, crossing his arms over his chest as if it weren't anything new to him.

"What else do you want me to say, Jack?" I stepped toward him, my eyes never leaving his face. "Do you want me to admit I'm attracted to you? That even though we haven't slept together yet, I still see you as mine?"

The ice dragon didn't answer, so I took it a step further and touched his arm, causing his icy gaze to fall on me.

"Because I do. Both of you are mine." I darted a look at Raiden who smiled and urged me on with a wave of his hand. I didn't linger on him because Jack was the one who needed my attention right now.

Finally, it seemed like I broke something in him because he placed a hand on my cheek and stroked my face with his thumb. "But you are more his than mine. I cannot compete with the physical pull he has."

"It isn't that." I shook my head, not wanting to think of myself as either of theirs. "Raiden and I have clicked from the beginning. He's been open with me. Trying to get to know me and yes, while he does have a slight physical advantage over you, you could be just as attractive to me if you tried."

His eyes widened slightly and then narrowed. "So you would lay with me right now?" His words made me go still, and as he raked his eyes over my body, he snorted. "Would you do it with Raiden in the room, or would you send him away? Perhaps you would ask him to join us?" The anger in his voice sliced through me. Jack's word hurt and even worse pissed me off. I wasn't doing this because I wanted to and here he was making it seem like everything was my fault. That I was the puppet master pulling the strings.

"What's your problem?" I growled, dropping my hands from the ice dragon. "Why the hell are you here?"

I had a bad habit. One which had gotten me in more trouble than naught. Whenever my feelings were hurt, I didn't cry or run away. Instead, I got angry. Which meant I said things I didn't mean. This was one of those times.

Hurt crossed Jack's face, and as I opened my mouth to apologize, to take it back, Raiden spoke. "Why don't you guys go on the tour together?" He smiled. "Seems you guys could stand to have some time alone." He yawned, stretching. "I could use a nap, anyway."

"What?" Jack asked irritation coloring his face. "How will that help any? She clearly expects us to share her in every aspect." He shivered. "I'm not sure that is something I can abide." He shook his head.

"No, I don't," I argued, glaring at him. While the thought of the two sharing me sexually made my blood race, sharing them emotionally all the time might be more than I could handle. Plus confusing as all get out.

"Then prove it," Raiden said, gesturing between the two of us. "Spend time with Jack alone and show him he still has a chance with you." Raiden placed a hand on each of our shoulders and gave us a little shove toward the door. "It's that, or we let you fight it out. Though, I think Lord Amun wouldn't be too happy about his room getting trashed."

Sighing in defeat, I offered a hand to Jack. "I guess, we might as well try. What would it hurt?"

Jack stared down at my hand as if it were a hissing viper. Then after a few seconds too long, he placed his large hand in mine.

My brows furrowed in question, and he offered me a small smile. "As you said, it couldn't hurt."

11

The silence could kill a monk. While Jack had agreed to give this "getting to know each other" thing a chance, he sure wasn't trying too hard. Not that I really had any room to talk since I hadn't said more than a few words since we'd left the palace.

Raiden had been so much easier to deal with. I hadn't had to try with him. He had a way of getting under your skin and making a home there. A delicious body fulfilling home. A shiver ran down my spine in remembrance.

I wished things between Jack and me were that easy, but the ice dragon had some kind of hang up holding him back. I'd only met a few of his kind before, and while some of them had been a bit standoffish, none to this degree. Either he was really shy, had a huge stick up his butt, or someone had hurt him in the past. I honestly didn't know which one I preferred more. All of them would make getting to know him complicated and enough work that I would really have to be committed to deal with.

Nevertheless, I couldn't figure out what I was dealing with unless one of us took the lead. Since it didn't seem like Jack would be stepping up anytime soon, it had to be me.

"Look." I jerked on his hand, bringing us to a stop in the middle of the street. "There's no point in doing this if neither of us tries."

"Agreed."

"So, I suggest we start with something small. Something easy." I glanced around the market, which had transformed in a few short hours from a desolate ghost town to a lively street fair. A delicious smell hit my nose just as my eyes landed on a food vendor.

Without a word, I grabbed Jack's hand and pulled him over to the vendor. "For example, what kind of foods do you like?"

Jack eyeballed the meat sticks the vendor sold and gave an appreciative nod. I ordered two, eagerly bouncing on my heels as I waited for them. Just talking about food reminded me how long it had been since we had eaten last. I thought I might die of hunger before the man finally handed me two sticks.

I turned away from him after paying and offered Jack one. While I bit into mine right away, a euphoric moan coming from my mouth, Jack sniffed at his.

"What?" I asked around a mouthful of meaty goodness. "Is there something wrong with it?"

"No, I do not enjoy spicy foods." He stared at the meat for a moment.

"Oh, it's not hot. I promise." I sucked some of the juice off my fingers. Jack's eyes darted from the meat to my face. "Did I get sauce on my face?" I reached a hand up to try to find it causing Jack to chuckle.

"No, you do not have food on your face." He took a bite of his meat and chewed it around in his mouth for a moment before swallowing with a satisfied nod. "You were right, not spicy at all."

"See?" I smirked and started down the street. "I wouldn't lie to you about food."

"So, you'd lie about other things?" he asked,

and I stopped to argue with him until I saw the twinkle in his eyes.

"Why, Jack, are you teasing me?" I smiled up at him as I finished off the rest of my meal.

"Only sometimes." He took the stick from my hand and then threw his and mine in a nearby trash can.

As he returned, he glanced around. "What else would you like to try?"

"Um… I'm not sure," I inhaled a breath that smelled like all the best things in life, grease, and sugar.

"I'm partial to those." He pointed at a vendor across the way who was busy pouring balls of dough into a vat of oil. "They're fried and covered in honey."

"Well, how could I say no to that? Let's get some." I smiled at him, and he nodded, taking my hand and moving me across the way. I wasn't sure if he'd done it on purpose or not, but the whole way there all I could think about was the touch of his flesh on mine.

"Two please," Jack said, holding up two fingers at the diminutive old man behind the counter.

"Syrup or honey?" the old man asked as he

scooped off bits of fried dough and put them into paper trays.

"One of each," Jack said as he paid the man. "That way she can experience both types and see which is to her liking."

"I hear that." The old man chuckled as he looked over at me. "Sometimes it's hard to choose which you want, eh?"

With that, he handed Jack our treats, and I tried really hard not to dwell on his words.

"Try the honey first. You'll find that it's overly sweet at first. It hits you all at once, but after that, there's not a lot more to it. Simple. Effective. Delicious." He picked one of them up with his long, delicate fingers and offered it to me. "Now open wide."

I did as I was told, and he popped it into my mouth. It was as he said, sweet, almost too sweet, and very delicious, but as I chewed on it, I realized he was right. After the initial burst of flavor, there wasn't a lot more to it.

"Wow, it's really good, Jack. Sort of reminds me of Loukoumades." When Jack gave me a confused look, I waved a hand dismissively. "It's a Greek pastry back home."

"Ah." He shrugged. "I had forgotten you visited

the human food." He looked down at the pastries. "I've always heard they had bad food there, but if they have stuff like this, I may have to go myself."

"I'd be happy to show you around sometime. We could eat our way across the world." I smiled at him as he popped the Waesigar equivalent of a Loukoumade into his mouth.

"I would like that." He nodded. "But, until then, I still have the other to show you." He smiled. "I know, it's easy to forget about the syrup because you had the honey, but bear with me." He pulled one out and held it out to me. "You'll notice that it's less sweet, but there's more complexity to it. You can actually pick out the individual notes of the syrup and the pastry because it's less overpowering."

He was right. As the fried treat hit my tongue, I could taste the layers of the syrup. The earthiness of the tree it had come from combined with the sweetness to envelop my tongue in waves, that had I not been paying attention, I'd have missed. It made the whole thing seem more fulfilling, especially after the overwhelming sweetness of the honey.

It was strange because while I could have seen myself going through the entire bag of honey ones before I'd tried the syrup, now that I had, I found myself wanting the second one a bit more.

"Which do you like more?" Jack asked as we began walking along the street. He held both bags to me.

"Honestly, both, but I think I'd rather the syrup now. I may go back for the honey later, but it's too overwhelming to eat for an extended period."

He nodded and handed me the bag. We walked in silence again for a few moments and then Jack abruptly asked, "You don't know the effect you have on people, do you?"

"What do you mean?" I turned my gaze from a street performer who had just dropped all his juggling balls, to Jack. He had a curious expression on his face as if trying to decipher me.

"I mean, you don't seem to know how attractive you are to the males around you. Even now, you draw the attention of others." Jack inclined his head toward a few men who had stopped what they were doing to stare at us.

"No," I scoffed. "They aren't. They are staring because we are foreigners. I'm hardly what anyone would call a catch. I'm surprised you and Raiden even agreed to this fiasco in the first place."

"That is your father's words coming from your

mouth, not ours." The seriousness in Jack's voice intrigued me. "Not everyone thinks a woman should be one way or another." He did a sort of cute little shimmy with his shoulders as he spoke. "Sometimes the dragon does not pick the female because they have the best hips for birthing or the better archery score. Sometimes it's about more."

His words made a part of me giddy. I'd never been one for compliments, probably because I didn't receive many. The fact that Jack and Raiden saw more in me even if it was something frivolous made me smile.

"More?" I quirked a brow at him, intrigued. "And you think that's what I have, more?"

"Certainly." Jack nodded and stopped beside a table filled with different knickknacks.

Several couples lined the side; the women kept discussing how beautiful the jeweled keepsake boxes were. How the light glinted off the gems just right. They were clearly trying to get their mates to purchase one for them. I thought the boxes were all right but not very practical and easily breakable.

Then something caught my eye. Buried in the back of the table, hardly noticeable to anyone not looking for it was a fan. I reached out and withdrew it, opening it up to admire the delicate design in the pale blue material.

"Look," I held the fan up to Jack. "It matches your eyes."

Smiling softly, Jack took the fan from me and held it up to the owner of the stand. He gave the man several coins before giving the fan back to me.

"I wasn't asking you to buy it," I argued though I clutched the fan to my chest like something as precious as the jewels on the keepsake boxes.

"I know." He shrugged.

They were the last words he said to me as we headed back to the palace. My head spun at the mystery that was Jack. As an ice dragon, it only made sense he didn't care for spicy things. Even thinking of the way he hadn't touched the meat until I confirmed it made me smile. Then the way he stared at me while I cleaned my hand or his obsession with pastry. Finally, Jack's silly talk about me. Saying I had something more before buying me something I had barely shown any interest in.

Confusing.

We stopped at the bedroom door, neither of us going in. I think we didn't want the night to end, I know I didn't. In addition, I knew that going in the room would mean seeing Raiden and then all kinds of questions would ensue.

"I hope you are aware of my affection for you." Jack's sudden admission pulled me out of my own thoughts. "I might not be as open as Raiden, but I do care for you."

"I know." I ducked my head down, not meeting his eyes. Feelings had never been something I had been good at. I cared for Jack too. Maybe not as intensely as I did for Raiden, but something more subtle. When Jack wasn't a hormonal pain in the butt, he was like a cool balm after being left to die in the scorching desert. Something I deeply needed with my father breathing down my neck.

"I still wish to be in this race," Jack said, pulling my attention back to him.

"That's good to know." I murmured at the floor and then glanced up at him beneath my lashes. "I don't think I could do what Lord Amun wants us to do with only Raiden at my side. He might be powerful in his own right, but he's still…"

"A child." Jack filled in for me.

"A bit." I smiled.

We stared at the door as if it were some kind of barrier between the real world and us. Then as if we had rehearsed it, we both turned from the door and spoke.

"I'm glad we did this," Jack said, and I said, "What now?"

Laughing at ourselves, Jack gestured for me to go first.

"I guess this is goodnight." I shifted from foot to foot, awkwardness starting to settle in.

"I suppose it is," Jack replied and then when my hand reached out to touch the doorknob his hand landed on mine. I watched as he drew it away from the door and brought it to touch his chest. I had no choice but to step toward him or have my arm jerked off.

It brought us inches from each other, and suddenly the awkward tension changed into something else. I placed the other hand still clasping my fan beside the other one putting me even closer to him. Our breath mingled between us and my eyes lashes fluttered closed just as his lips descended onto mine.

Jack didn't need any direction this time. His mouth covered mine, and he wasted no time, swiping his tongue at my lips asking them to part. I needed little provocation, more than ready to let my feelings out and greedily accepted him. His hands came around my waist settling low on my hips. Jack applied a slight amount of pressure, which caused my thighs to press together in need.

The scent must have hit Jack's nose because my back hit the wall beside the door moments later. One hand tangled in his long hair and the other clutched onto the fan for dear life as he devoured every inch of my mouth.

Small mewing sounds came from my throat, and I knew I was coming close to the no-stopping-zone. Jack must have noticed because he dragged himself away, but my mouth tried to keep him there, causing him to laugh. It was a genuine laugh, low and husky. One that told me he knew exactly how he affected me.

"We must stop," he said, smoothing my hair away from my face before placing his forehead against mine.

"I know." I breathed. The slight whine in my voice making me wince.

"You made me think you did not want me but now..." He ground his hips against me making me gasp. I wasn't the only one who affected by something as simple as a kiss.

"I never said that." I leaned my head back against the wall so I could look up into his eyes.

"I know. It was my own jealousy getting in the way." Shame covered Jack's face, and I had the urge to kiss him again before he smirked. "I thought this would be easy. That you would take one look at me and know who was the better dragon."

"I'm sorry?" I offered not sure what else to say.

"It's not your fault." He shook his head. "The women back home are much more easily wooed, and I just didn't expect I'd actually have to work for your affections."

"I feel like that was supposed to be a compliment," I said, trying really hard not to get annoyed with him. Had he really expected me to just fall all over him?

"It was, and you should take it as so." Jack moved away from me, so the hard front of him didn't press against me anymore. A part of me disliked being apart already which I could only take as a good sign.

We were silent for a moment, and then I took a step toward the door once more. "I guess we should go inside. Raiden will probably be wondering where we are."

Before I could get to the door, Jack grabbed my hand again. I thought maybe he wanted another kiss, and while I wasn't entirely against it, I knew it would only lead to an embarrassing situation if someone happened to walk by us in the open hallway.

But he didn't.

Jack leaned down until his mouth brushed my ear and whispered, "I may not get to bed you tonight but be warned. I will claim your body as mine, and when I do, no dragon will be able to stand against us."

I swallowed hard at his words. If I had been human on Earth and a man said this to me, I'd have screamed about not belonging to anyone, but this wasn't Earth, and I wasn't human. The dragon inside of me roared at his claim and urged me to let him try right there in the hallway where everyone could see us.

I shoved her down and then met Jack's eyes with a coy grin. "I look forward to it."

12

Raiden didn't say anything when we had arrived in the room nor when we'd lain down for the night. The bed had been big enough to fit all three of us without having to touch each other. However, it didn't stop me from thinking about it.

To say it had been a restless night would be an understatement.

"Do you think this Firestar is a formidable opponent?" Jack asked as we finished packing the rest of our belongings up the next morning.

My shoulders tensed. "I'm not sure." My voice came out shaking, and I hoped they didn't notice my reaction.

"I heard the Southern Lord's son had the

highest kill count in the last war," Raiden commented, leaning against the edge of the bed. He had been on his best behavior since the woods. Trying to help me out with Jack. Even keeping his hands to himself the entire night when I had been sure he would try something the moment Jack went to sleep. Either he was overconfident in his place amongst this little trio, or he didn't think Jack was a threat. Either way, it was worrisome.

Raiden and Jack weren't fighting, and I could hardly complain, but how could he be so okay with sharing me? I, myself, was finding it a bit hard to swallow even if I was the one who was getting all the benefit. I hoped his laid-back personality was real and not some coping mechanism that was going to blow up in my face later.

"Really?" Jack asked, raising a brow. "I had not heard such a thing. Do you expect trouble?"

"I always expect trouble." Raiden shot Jack a grin. Their camaraderie made things easier for me but harder when it came time to pick the winner.

"It doesn't matter anyway," I interrupted their moment. "We can't leave until we defeat him or at least make him agree to stop."

"You think he will be willing to make a deal?" Raiden's expression turned to surprise.

I shrugged. "I don't know. Maybe. We'll have to try something. Three against a whole army isn't great odds."

My words caused the other two to go silent. We finished packing and met Herbert at the front gate. After he informed me he had been given a bed in the servant's quarters, I filled him in on the new plans.

"I also think you should stay behind." I clapped Herbert on the shoulder. "This isn't a simple political trip anymore. We can't guarantee your safety."

"What kind of dragon would I be if I left you now?" Herbert shook his head, and the fierceness in his eyes surprised me.

Thankfully, Jack stepped in, keeping me from having to break the older man's heart. "No one is questioning your honor. What I believe Maya is trying to say, is we could move faster if you would stay behind."

When Herbert looked to me for confirmation, I nodded vigorously. "I'm sure you would be great in battle but with your arm…"

"I'd just slow you down." Herbert sighed in defeat. "I understand. I will wait with bated breath for your return."

I smiled at the driver, patting him on the arm.

"We'll be back as soon as we can." I dropped my hand with a frown. I said the words to comfort Herbert, but I didn't believe them, not one bit. Firestar wasn't a "one and done" kind of dragon. He was more of a "down in the flames of glory" kind. Which was bad for everyone all around. Including me.

Worse, the direction to the volcanoes was vague at best, but luckily, the monstrous mountaintops weren't hard to miss.

Since we didn't have the carriage anymore, the trek took longer than it would have. I had to admit I had gotten soft in my time on Earth. I wasn't as fast as I used to be or as stealthy. But I hadn't really had to be. If I needed to get somewhere quickly, I simply took a cab or the subway, and when it came to stealth, there really wasn't much call for it as a computer engineer. Not unless I was game testing and then the virtual world took care of it for me. Sadly, those skills did not transfer over to me.

After the sixth time I tripped over a tree root, Raiden called us to stop. Groaning, I flopped down on the ground. I didn't want to seem weak in front of them, but I couldn't be more thankful for the break. My feet were killing me. Running on a treadmill had nothing on hiking. I really should have taken better care of myself while on Earth, but I hadn't expected to come home so soon, if ever. Now, my feet were hating me for it.

"Maybe you should let one of us carry you. Then we could fly the rest of the way?" Raiden suggested, pulling out a flask of water and passing it around the group.

I shook my head before I drank from the container. The water soothed my parched throat, and I sighed. "No, they'll see us if we come from above. We have to stay on foot. They won't be expecting it."

"Agreed." Jack nodded, taking the water from me. "We will have a better chance to survey the threat if we are undetected."

He tipped the container back and drank from it, but some of it slipped from the side and slid down his throat. Even in my tired and worn out state, I could still appreciate the long line of his neck and the expansion of his muscles. While I'd seen more than my share of Raiden's spectacular body, I had yet to get even a glimpse of what Jack had to offer. After last night's kiss, I could safely say I was more than a little giddy to find out.

"This is going to take forever." Raiden threw his

head back and groaned, snapping me out of my little fantasy.

"Well, sorry," I growled, more upset that I had been fantasizing than Raiden's whining. "I haven't had much need to trek through the woods while on Earth. There aren't that many chances of being attacked either."

"Oh yeah, I forgot." Raiden grinned sheepishly, rubbing the back of his multi-toned head. "What's it like over there, anyway? Your father never let you answer."

"It's different," I mused, not really wanting to get into it. Talking about it only made me miss it more. Which I found ironic since I had hated it from the moment I stepped into the dimension. Funny how that worked out.

"Oh, that's a lot of information please slow down." Raiden teased, making me grin.

I didn't answer him even with his jokes, but when he only stared at me waiting for an answer, I sighed. "Fine. You want to know?"

"Please." Raiden leaned his elbows on his knees as eager as a kid having his first flying lesson. Not that I would know. My wings still hadn't graced me with their presence. Part of me hoped this little adventure would suddenly make them sprout up. Though, it was a small hope.

Jack shifted at my side, coming a bit closer. The pure focus in his eyes made my heart jump in my chest a little. He placed his hand on my knee as if to make sure he had my full attention before asking in a low voice, "I, too, wish to know. So far, all you've mentioned is that the food is excellent."

Well, how could I say no to that?

You can't, a dreamy part of me replied.

The problem now was where to start? I could tell them so much. The food, the clothing. While there are similarities between our two worlds, Waesigar relied on magic, and while it had limitations, it didn't have as many as science did. I thought of telling them about Ryan and Bianca, but a selfish part of me wanted to keep something for myself. I already had to give away so much for this world. My body. My future. If I could keep one thing, it would be them. Then again, I might not ever see them again.

"It's not like here," I finally said, but before I could get any further into it, Raiden interrupted me.

"Obviously," he snorted and readjusted his feet.

I made a noise in my throat and glared at him. "Do you want me to tell you or not?"

"Sorry, sorry." He held his hands up in defense before mimicking a zipper across his lips. "My lips are sealed."

"Good." I nodded and settled in to tell them all about my life on Earth. "I know my father spread the lie that I was in some prestigious group to study abroad, but it's not even close. In truth, they dumped me in the middle of some human city without a clue as to what to do next."

"You mean they just left you all by yourself?" Raiden asked. His mouth dropped open, and his eyes widened, showing his disbelief.

I nodded with a frown. "They gave me the documents I needed to be over there, of course. So I wasn't completely helpless, but I might as well have been."

"Documents?" Jack raised a brow. "You need documentation to live somewhere?"

I chuckled. "Crazy right?" The guys nodded in agreement as they tried to wrap their heads around that little bit of knowledge. If that part blew their minds, the next one would be a game changer. "They have to keep track of people somehow. It's not like here. You can't just pop between countries without permission. They say it's because they'd have a hard time tracking down criminals and the like."

"Why can't they just send a messenger to all the kingdoms and have them track them down?" Raiden waved a hand in the air. "That's how we captured Melona."

"Melona?" I glanced at Jack to see if he knew what Raiden was talking about.

"Melona was an ice dragon from two years ago. You weren't here," Jack explained, his mask firmly in place. "He killed twenty-four others before he was finally caught trying to sneak into the Eastern Region."

"Yeah!" Raiden jumped in with a shout. "It was great. I got to help with the interrogation."

The lightning dragon was a bit more enthusiastic than I would have been at the prospect of torture. Something I didn't expect from the easygoing guy. However, if his bedroom self told me anything, there was more to Raiden than just a boyish smile.

"So what else?" Raiden prompted, the excitement flashing in his eyes. "Why all the crazy control? Last I heard, they weren't under some kind of tyrant."

My lips curled up into knowing smile. "Well, you try keeping track of billions of people without all hell breaking loose."

"Did she just say billions?" Raiden gaped, shaking his head.

Jack nodded his own mask coming down briefly from his shock. "I believe she did, though I hardly believe it."

"Where do they put them all?" I smiled at Raiden's question as he tried to comprehend what I had told him.

"They have lots of buildings. So tall they block out the sun." I raised my hand high above me. It had shocked me as well when I first arrived. The big cities. The crowds of people shoving each other as they try to get to where they were going. It had taken a lot to get used to.

"That sounds…" Raiden trailed off, and Jack finished for him. "Claustrophobic."

Laughing at their description, I couldn't help but agree. It had been a bit like that. It took me weeks to get used to the air and the sky. Once I had figured out how to call a ride, the first place I had gone was to the countryside. It was only then, when the stars were shining down on me, that I had been able to breathe. My many trips out there had been the only things keeping me sane while I learned to blend into my new home.

Now the quiet of Waesigar was strange to me. I hoped it didn't take as long to adapt to being back in Waesigar than it had taken to adjust to Earth. With any luck, I wouldn't have to find out.

"Do you miss it?" Jack asked so suddenly, I thought maybe he might have read my mind, but the curiousness in his gaze assured me he hadn't.

"Very much so," I murmured, staring down at the ground. "You already know I wasn't brought back by choice, and if I had my say in it, I wouldn't have come back at all."

"Then why did you?" Raiden's question held a hint of accusation in it I didn't like.

I leveled my gaze at him and sighed, "You've met my father. Do you really think he would let me stay when they needed me so desperately?"

"Then why do you stay?" Jack prodded, his face guarded. "Why did you agree to this if your heart was not in it? Do you have someone back on Earth? A lover?"

Raiden seemed to catch on to what Jack had asked and his gaze settled on my face as he waited for my answer as well. It took me a moment to realize they were jealous and possibly a bit hurt.

Who could blame them? Here they were trying to woo me, and I didn't really want to be wooed. However, I had done a good job hiding my discomfort for this whole thing. I had slept with Raiden after all.

I sighed and rubbed my hands over my eyes. Things were getting complicated. They would be even worse once we reached Firestar. I couldn't see that going any way but bad.

"Well?" Raiden urged me on. There was an insecurity in his question, which made my heart ache. I didn't want to hurt him, either of them. Thankfully, I didn't have to lie about this one.

"No, there was no one on Earth." As I finally answered, they both seemed to relax. "That's not to say there weren't people there I care for though. I had friends. A job. I'd just achieved something really big right before I got jerked out of there and forced back into all of this." I gestured around the circle of our little camp.

"Then what's keeping you from going back?" Jack raised a brow. "We certainly aren't stopping you."

"Well, I..." the words stuttered out, and I found myself embarrassed at the only answer I had. "I don't exactly know how to open a portal on my own, and besides, I have you guys now."

"What about us?" Raiden eased forward closer to me. "Finding someone to make you a portal shouldn't be that hard. There's plenty of people who are skilled in such magic."

"Maybe I don't want to leave right now." I snapped, not liking the interrogation. I wanted to leave sure, but other things were going on now, and my conflicting emotions were giving me a headache. I needed to be done with this conversation.

"Maybe it would be better if we kept going?" Jack, ever the insightful one, suggested.

He climbed to his feet and held a hand out to me. I handed Raiden back his water jug before taking it. Pulling me up, I found myself closer to him than I expected. My eyes darted to his lips and last night's events came rushing to the front of my mind. Licking my own lips, I let out a shuddering breath.

"I think that would be a good idea," I said, stepping back from Jack.

Raiden and Jack exchanged a knowing grin, which only added to my irritation. I rolled my eyes and didn't wait for them to start moving before I headed toward volcano valley.

I made a conscious effort to not trip over anything and thankfully, managed only to fall a few times. Each time Raiden or Jack was there to catch me, their hands wrapping around me, caressing my body more than they needed to. By the time we arrived on the outskirts of Firestar's camp, I was a ball of quivering need.

"Are you all right?" Raiden asked with a condescending smile. "Do you need help with anything?"

"Yes," Jack added, stroking his fingers along my cheek. "We are happy to help you in any way possible."

Oh, I bet they were. My pulsating need only added to my irritation, and I jerked away from Jack and Raiden's touch with a glare.

"We have a job to do, and if you know what's good for you, you'll stop teasing me." My beast let out a low warning growl as I stomped over to a bundle of bushes. I ignored the chuckles coming from the men behind me and focused on the scene in front of me.

A dozen or so tents were set up around a clearing. More dragon warriors like those who had attacked us in the woods prowled the camp. Some practiced with their weapons in an arena while others cheered them on. Those who weren't at the arena were cleaning weapons or doing other daily tasks. It all seemed so normal, it was hard to believe they were bad guys.

"There has to be at least twenty or more." Raiden came up beside me and looked through the bushes with me. "What are we going to do?"

Jack stepped up beside us, peering over my shoulder. "We can't just rush in. We might be able to take out a few, but we would never reach this Firestar person before getting caught. I suggest we wait until nightfall and use the cover of darkness to sneak through the camp. Then hopefully, we will be able to surprise him in his bed."

"It's a good of a plan as any." I sighed, clapping my hands on my knees as I prepared to stand, but a tap on my shoulders topped me. The sharp end of a sword met my gaze, and I followed it from my shoulder until I reached the form holding the weapon.

Dressed in the same clothing as the men who had attacked us in the woods, the dragon with the sword stood in front of a dozen others.

13

We didn't even try to fight them. The likelihood we would win was considerably low, even with Raiden's new trident. Instead, we let them march us out of our hiding spot and into the middle of the camp.

There were a few catcalls shot my way, which I responded to with a special one-finger salute. The men hadn't bothered to bind our hands, but they did surround Jack and Raiden so completely, I almost couldn't see them.

"Hey," I cried out when they started to lead them to a different tent. "Where are you taking them?"

"Our lord will want to see you," one of the men

informed me as he took me by the arm and led me to a large tent.

"Screw that," I muttered, and as he raised a curious eyebrow at me, I kicked him in the knee. The sound of tearing cartilage filled my ears as a shriek of pain burst from his lips. As he crumpled to the ground gripping his knee, I darted for Jack and Raiden.

The sky overhead began to crackle, and lightning split the horizon. Thunder cracked so loud, I could feel it in the pit of my stomach. A wave of frost swept outward, fast-freezing the two guards on Jack's left right before a bolt of lightning shattered them into bloody chunks.

As bits of guard rained down around them, I saw the flash of Raiden's trident. He swung it through the air, driving the guards backward, funneling them away. For a moment, I was confused, but as the first of them slipped, I realized Jack had frozen the ground behind the guards.

"Maya, stay back!" Raiden called, right before he drove his trident into the ground. The Lightning traveled along the frozen earth before leaping up over the guards. Their bodies spasmed, muscles locking together as they crumpled to the ground in smoke-filled heaps.

"Get back here," the guard behind me cried, and I spun to see him back on his feet. His face was lined with pain as he flew toward me on wings of flame.

I drew on my powers, pulling the vines from the earth and gestured toward him. They wrapped around his injured leg and pulled. An earsplitting shriek filled the air as his wings faltered and he crashed to the ground like a bag of wet cement. I whipped my hand out, and my vines wrapped around him, binding him to the earth and holding him in place.

More men rushed out of the surrounding tents, and while some were dressed for battle, most were bare-chested in a way that made me think we'd awoken them. Even still, they charged toward us as I moved beside Raiden and Jack.

My two men quickly sandwiched me, blocking me from the coming attacks with their bodies. I never imagined I'd be standing here between an army and the two men who had suddenly come into my life. The two men, who had become so much more to me than just a pair of suitors my father had chosen for me. I didn't know which one I would choose or if I even would, but at that moment, it didn't matter. I just knew deep in my gut my place was there between them and anyone who would try to separate us. Even if that meant dying in the process.

Raiden stood in front, his trident gleaming, and Jack stood just behind, his hands glowing with frost magic, and that was when I realized how they'd won so quickly. They were fighting together with Jack using his ice magic to slow the enemies while Raiden finished them off.

Oddly enough, as the bandits surged toward us, they seemed to realize that while they could overwhelm us, they'd be unlikely to succeed without taking even more casualties. A tense silence filled the battlefield before a half-naked man with a flaming tattoo emblazoned across his chest strode forward. He gripped a massive sword in one hand, and as his eyes raked over us, he sighed.

"Our orders are not to harm you, but if you don't come quietly, we might just have to go against them." He gestured behind him toward what had to be over a dozen archers. "Your magic is formidable, but will you be able to fight back when we blot out the sky with arrows?"

"Are you sure?" Raiden asked, his trident crackling in his hands. "Because my buddy here is pretty sure he can stop all of them before they even fire. Isn't that right, Jack?"

"Yes." Jack nodded solemnly, his hands glowing white with unspent ice magic. "I will shatter their hands before they even pull back their bowstrings, and even if I do somehow miss one, Raiden commands lightning. The whole of the sky will protect us."

"Then we are at an impasse because our lord very much wants to speak with you." He met my eyes. "Privately." The man's expression darkened. "If you do not come peaceably, we will make this happen, and this time, I will not have my men hold back."

As he spoke, something about his words made my heart tingle. Had Firestar known I, specifically, was coming? I wasn't sure, but either way, I had little doubt Firestar wouldn't hurt me.

"I'll meet your lord, but they have to come with me." I gripped Raiden and Jack's arms, taking a step back so I could stand between them. My touch caused a low growl to come from both of them, their inner dragons not liking the threat before us.

"Fine," the guard conceded. "But one wrong move, and you will find yourselves wishing you had let her go alone."

Raiden's hand tightened on his trident, and he didn't put it away, not even when we were led to a large tent or when we entered it.

"Are you trying to burn the tent down around us?" A voice called out from deep within the tent. A voice I knew very well.

I nodded at Raiden, and with a flick of his wrist, the trident vanished, melding into the skin of his forearm like a glowing, golden tattoo. The lamp in the middle of the dimly lit tent didn't light the whole area, leaving half the tent shrouded in darkness.

"Hello, Maya," Firestar's voice rumbled from the darkness, making goosebumps appear on my skin and my blood to race through my veins.

"It's been a long time, Firestar." I strained to see him through the shadows, but he stayed hidden from my view.

"You know this man?" Jack asked from my side, and I forced myself not to wince at the accusation there.

"Yes, we have met before." I didn't embellish on how well we knew each other and hoped Firestar would have the decency to not fill in the blanks.

"That's why you were acting funny when Lord Amun told us who the bandit leader was," Raiden mused though he didn't sound as upset as Jack did.

"I never thought I'd see you again," Firestar commented as if the other two men didn't exist. He moved closer to the edge of the light, allowing me to see his silhouette. Large and muscled, Firestar's size had always been something I appreciated. He'd never tried to intimidate me, instead he had made me feel safe and secure.

"I didn't either," I commented after a moment. It was true. I hadn't thought I'd ever see him after he'd been sent away and I'd been banished to the human world.

His hands clasped together in front of him, and I could see the tension in his body from here. "I thought you were banished."

"Heh," I smiled slightly, "it didn't stick."

"Your father finally pull his head out of his ass?" His question caused the men at my side to tense, and I knew they were beginning to catch on that I knew him a bit more than I had let on.

The visual made my smile broaden, and I shook my head. "Never."

"I heard about your sister. I am sorry." Firestar shook his head in the shadows. "She didn't deserve such a fate."

"No one does," Raiden added with a bit of defiance. Maybe he wasn't as okay with my lie as I had believed.

The fact that Firestar knew about Aeis's misfortune was news to me. I didn't know the goings on in our region had reached this far. I wondered what else he knew.

"And who are these men?" He gestured to Raiden and Jack. "You needed bodyguards to come see me?"

I opened my mouth to answer, but nothing came out. I didn't know how to describe them. Did I introduce them as my friends? My potential mates? My lovers?

Unfortunately, during my internal war, Jack answered for me. "We are her suitors."

Firestar barked out laughing. "Really? This must be some kind of joke. That blowhard rejected me but thinks these guys are better? I can't believe you would agree to that."

Thinking about the two men my father had chosen for me I could see how he would like them better than Firestar. Jack had a cool calm about him that kept him level-headed in political situations. Raiden, on the other hand, was so laid back, I didn't think there was much of anything that could faze him. Together they were a dynamic duo who made Firestar, a known hot head, seem like an impossible choice.

I shrugged. "Wasn't really given a choice in the matter."

This caused him to cross his arms over his chest. Even in the shadows, I could see the muscle bulge beneath his skin. Largely built, the thin layer of fat from indulging in too much wine only made him that much more of an intimidating size.

"And what do you think of this?" he asked, nodding his head to Jack and Raiden who were not becoming any happier the longer we were there. Firestar did always have a way of pulling the truth from me.

"We both came willingly, knowing what we were getting into," Raiden answered for them both.

"And what exactly is that?" Firestar asked his gaze focused on the lightning dragon. "What are you getting into?"

"The first one to get Maya pregnant gets to be Lord of the Western lands." This came from Jack who had put on his cool mask of indifference.

Firestar guffawed. "Listen to him. A perfect little lap dog for your father to control. Please tell me you haven't fucked him yet?"

"And if I have?" I growled not liking how he talked about Jack.

"I might just have to kill him," Firestar said as he stepped into the light letting me see the feral grin on his lips.

My heart jumped into my throat. Firestar hadn't changed one bit. An arrogant chin accompanied his light brown eyes and flaming red hair. The only noticeable difference and, even most wouldn't have noticed, was his hair.

"You cut your hair." The words suddenly came out of my mouth, all thoughts of him killing Jack and Raiden flying from my mind.

His hand reached up to touch his shortened locks sticking straight up on his head. "Only a little bit, I remember how much you liked to hold onto it during…" he trailed off, giving me a roguish grin.

My face heated more.

"So you don't just know this man, do you, Maya?" Jack's words jerked me out of my little fantasy world and back to reality. Right, we weren't alone. Things from the past should stay there in the past.

"Oh?" Firestar's eyes lit up, and the grin on his lips grew. "Your dear princess didn't tell you how she knew me before she dragged you out here?" I stared at my feet as neither of them replied, which was answer enough. Firestar laughed, so pleased with himself I could punch him. "Oh, then please let me enlighten you."

"Please do," Jack's tone held enough ice to freeze the whole western hemisphere. All the progress I had made with him had gone down the drain in an instant.

"I really don't think that is necessary." I tried to object, but the men ignored me.

"Maya and I were lovers." Firestar stated, letting it sink in before adding, "In fact, we were more than lovers. We were to be married." My eyes snapped to Firestar in irritation. We had talked about being married but never got that far. My father had shut it down faster than I could say corsage.

"Except her father didn't approve," Raiden interjected, his eyes sliding up and down Firestar with disdain. "I can see why not."

Firestar frowned and then hollered, "Blorder!"

The guard from before came in with three other men. "Yes, my lord?"

"Show these two where they will be staying tonight. I wish to speak to the princess alone." His eyes locked with mine and a shudder went through me.

"No, we aren't leaving." Raiden jerked away from Blorder as he tried to lead him away.

"It's fine, Raiden." I placed a hand on his arm, but he shot me a scathing look, which shot straight into my heart. "Nothing will happen, I promise."

Raiden shrugged off my hand and turned away. "Why should I care, just one more opponent in a long race." Before he left the tent, he turned back with a nasty grin. "Don't forget, Princess, I've already got a head start." Then he and Jack disappeared through the tent door without another word.

Sighing, I relaxed slightly before turning back to Firestar. "Why'd you have to do that?"

"What? Them?" He gestured to the exit. "Don't worry about them. They'll get over it when they realize they don't have a chance with you."

"Says who?" I scowled.

"Says me."

Turning the attention away from me and back to him, I nodded at the brown pants, which hung loosely on his legs and the dark gray shirt with red lacing. "I see your sense of style hasn't changed. You've even got an army following suit."

Firestar chuckled and scratched the back of his head. "It wasn't on purpose, believe me."

"I know." I nodded with a smile and then took a step away from him. We were being too friendly. Too easily falling into the same banter from long before. That wasn't good, not when I had a job to do, anyway.

"As much as I hate to say it, I'm not here on a social call." I waited for Firestar to explode or tell me he knew since, somehow, he knew so much already.

Instead, he walked over to the small table where he had a pitcher of wine and a plate of cheese. He poured two glasses, setting one on the other side of the table before sitting down in the opposite chair. He gestured for me to sit.

Frowning as I debated whether I should, my attention jerked back to the cry of pain from outside the tent. Brow furrowed, I said, "If I sit with you will you call your dogs off?"

"Done." Firestar quipped and then yelled, "Blorder!"

The guard from before, the one who had offered to scratch my itch appeared in the tent doorway. "Yes, my lord?"

"If any hair is out of place on my woman's

men, I will have your balls for a necklace." The calm tone of Firestar's voice as he threatened his guard would make even my father quake in his boots.

Blorder's eyes widened, and he bowed deeply mumbling, "Yes, my lord." Then he turned tail and ran out of the tent as if the devil himself chased him. For all I knew, he might be.

I could hear Blorder yelling at someone, and then there was a commotion and then silence. Satisfied Raiden and Jack wouldn't be harmed — at least not any further — I approached Firestar and sat at the table. I picked up the glass but didn't drink from it.

"So how have you been, Maya?" Firestar asked, drinking heavily from his glass. His eyes never left my face the entire time.

"As well as can be when you're banished to another dimension," I tried to keep the bitterness out of my voice, but the frown on Firestar's lips said I failed. Time for a change of subject. "What about you? Why are you…?" I gestured around the tent.

Firestar's gaze hardened. "Many things have changed since your father kicked me out."

"He hardly kicked you out," I scoffed. "You got mad and stormed out."

"You would do the same if he had said those things about you," Firestar growled before filling his cup once more. "Unworthy hot head my right wing."

"That aside, who knows what might have happened if you had stayed." I gently reminded him. "We could have made it work even without my father's blessing."

"Ha!" Firestar threw one hand up in the air. "That was unlikely. He had you out of there before the dust had even settled on my departure and now he's whored you out to the highest bidder."

Anger filled me at his description. "I would hardly call it whoring."

"They get something out of it, don't they? Get the chance to be the next Lord of the Western Lands if they can get you pregnant." He gestured rudely at my abdomen.

"And what exactly are you doing?" I asked, gripping the cup in my hands tight. "Why are you here Firestar? Fighting against your own lands, your own father."

Firestar shook his head a bit dejected. "I told you, things have changed. My father isn't who he pretends to be. He doesn't have the heart of the people in mind."

"And you do by robbing them of what little they have?" I snapped back, banging my cup on the table.

Firestar sighed, "I'm not stealing from anyone. It's father who's the real criminal. The one you should be here to stop is him."

14

The confidence in Firestar's voice made it hard for me to pretend what he said was a delusion. He really thought his father, Lord Amun, was the bad guy here. Why would the guy who put me here in the first place be the one in the wrong? I mean, he was the one with a city full of scared people and a palace barer than a mausoleum. Then there was the worst part of it all. If he was, did that mean I was too?

"What do you mean your father is stealing from the people?" I leaned forward in my chair as I tried to wrap my head around the notion. "He said you were the thief."

"No, it's not me." Firestar shook his head from the seat across from me. There was a sadness in his eyes I couldn't shake, but if he was telling the truth, there were some things that didn't make sense. Like the attack in the woods.

"Then why are you holed up here with the same guys who attacked us in the woods? Didn't you want to stop us from reaching him?" I waved a hand in front of me as I pressed my lips together in confusion. This whole thing was just giving me a headache.

Firestar reached out and took my hand in his. My body jolted at his touch, and an electric fizzle went through me. I had to give it to him. He still had that magic touch.

His eyes softened as his fingers stroked my hand, each touch causing a tingle to run through me. "I would never hurt you, Maya. You mean too much to me to let any harm come to you. Besides," his hand tightened on mine as his eyes hardened, "I didn't know you were here until one of my spies saw you in the market with that ice dragon. What's his name?"

"Who?" I asked not really knowing what he was talking about. Like when we first met, his very touch caused all sensibility to leave my head, and it took some effort to finally focus. Shaking my head clear of the fog, I cleared my throat and said, "Jack, his name is Jack." A silvery white head of hair came to mind as I withdrew my hand from Firestar's. I couldn't let myself be distracted. I had a job to do. Even though, I wasn't quite sure I should be doing it now. While Firestar hadn't lied to me before, it'd been years since we had seen each other and people change.

"You care for him, don't you?" Firestar raised a surprised brow. "It's not just about having an heir. You genuinely have feelings for him, for Jack."

"Possibly," I mumbled and leaned back in my chair and crossed my arms over my chest as I looked away from his prodding gaze. I so didn't want to talk about my feelings with my ex-lover. I still hadn't wrapped my head around what I wanted from the two men waiting outside, let alone the one in front of me.

"And the other one?" he asked with a violent jerk of his cup. "Do you care for him too? Or have you already chosen?"

"No. I haven't chosen anyone yet." And I might not, I added to myself. My heart still didn't know what it wanted. Part of me still wanted to be back on Earth working on my next game project while the other half of me wanted nothing more than to wrap myself around the two men who had wiggled their way into my life and my blood.

"He doesn't seem to think so," Firestar taunted me, reminding me of what Raiden had said before he left. Oh, what Firestar must think of me? "Does he know how you like it?" The question was so out of left field, I flushed in response. "Does he know about the place behind your ear that if you kiss it just right will make you go on the spot?"

"Stop it," I hissed, crossing one leg over the other. His words were crude, but to my shame, they were causing my body to remember how it had been between us. How it could be again.

"What? Afraid I will mess up your little triad?" Firestar brought his cup up to his mouth, but I could still see the smug grin on his lips at the edge.

"No, because you aren't in the running." I looked down at my shoes as I said it. Truth be told, he wasn't in the running, but what if he wanted to be? What would I do then? I wasn't sure, and that bugged me more than anything else.

"I could be." He countered, the arrogance in his face almost too much to bear. Now, I remembered why my father disliked him. While Firestar could easily draw someone in with his charms, his ability to do so made him overconfident. That quality didn't always make for a good leader. It caused good men to die from rash decisions, men like my brother.

Still, I found myself contemplating his offer anyway because part of me had missed him all these years. Still, the logical side reminded me why I sat here in the first place.

"We were talking about your father, not about me," I reminded him, and I was damned pleased I kept the tremor of desire out of my voice.

"We can do both." He chuckled and stretched his arms out above his head. It made his shirt stretch out across his chest, and suddenly, I was an eighteen-year-old girl again. My mouth watered and my hormones raged. I wanted nothing more than to climb across the table and ride him until we both exploded.

"You win." I sighed and shook my head. "I'm still attracted to you. I want you as much as I did before you ran off. Are you happy now?"

"Hardly," Firestar scoffed but dropped his arms down to his side. "But the men who attacked you were impostors. My father's men disguised as mine to make you think I was the one doing it when, in reality, it is he who doesn't want you here."

Brow furrowed, I tilted my glass back and forth

on the table. It made some sense. It would explain why my father hadn't been able to get a response. Lord Amun probably doesn't want to renew the alliance, and when my father sent us, Lord Amun tried to get rid of us. If that were true, why would he do it?

"Why doesn't your father want to keep the alliance? Do you know?" I leaned forward on my elbows, hoping Firestar could fill in the blanks. I wasn't sure why, but I trusted him to tell me the truth, foolish as that might have been.

Firestar shrugged. "More than likely he doesn't want your father or the other lords to find out about what he's doing."

"And what exactly is he doing? You said he stole from the people." I repeated his words back to him, trying to figure out the bigger picture. "How and the bigger question here, why?"

"I found out he has a huge debt. Like, enormous." He spread his arms wide. "The last war cost us more than anyone knew, and he had taken out loans from some guy in the North. Now he has come to collect, but my father doesn't have the money. In fact, we are on the brink of poverty because of it." The sadness and shame in his face made my heart ache for him. Before I could stop myself, I reached over and clasped his hands in mine. Firestar gave me a small smile, squeezing my hands slightly in response.

"So, then why are you out here instead of in there trying to help fix it?" I cocked my head to the side not quite seeing how he ended up there.

Firestar sighed and let go of my hands. "I tried to approach him about it. Tell him it was wrong to steal from the people. He should just tell them what happened and raise the taxes temporarily until we can pay the debt back, but his pride refuses to listen to reason."

I nodded, understanding what pride can do to someone. My father had it in spades.

"Then when I threatened to tell them myself, he faked a robbery and blamed it on me." He rubbed his hand over his weary face. "He banished me in front of everyone for my 'crimes,' and now I'm lucky to have found a home here with the few loyal men I could convince to leave with me."

"And so you found your home between two volcanoes? Why didn't you just jump into one? It would have saved you time?" I pointed out sarcastically before standing from the table. Pacing back and forth, I rehashed everything he had told me. Lord Amun bad. Firestar good. Which left me where? Stuck in the middle of a complicated mess.

"As if I didn't have enough on my plate already," I muttered under my breath.

"What was that?" Firestar asked from his seat.

"Nothing." I waved him off. "Just trying to figure out how I'm going to get out of this mess."

Man, I thought coding the final boss of Waesigar had been hard. All the extra twists and turns we had to put in so players wouldn't get bored but would still be willing to spend all their precious time on it. It had been such a stressful time, Ryan had ended up on the other end of a tequila bottle, but unfortunately, I hadn't had that luxury. I did get a lovely video to post online of Ryan singing a hit pop song including a dance number. It had over ten thousand views online.

"What are you smiling about?" Firestar asked from right next to me causing me to jump in place.

"Don't do that," I snapped, clasping my hand over my racing heart.

"Sorry." Firestar grinned sheepishly and tucked a lock of hair behind my ear causing my heart to race for a whole different reason. "You're so beautiful. You know that, don't you?" The hand on my face cupped my cheek, his thumb tracing along the top of my lips.

"To you maybe." I bit my lower lip and stared down at the ground.

"No, not just to me." He placed his other hand on my cheeks, firmly trapping my face between his grasp. "Your father might have made you think you weren't desirable, but you are. Otherwise, how would you have gained the attention of not just one prince but two other noble dragons?"

"Just lucky I guess," I tried to joke, but it only made Firestar frown. Sighing, I withdrew myself from his grasp and moved away. "I know what you are saying, but it's hard to change how you see yourself when everyone has been telling you your whole life you aren't worthy. Now, all of a sudden, I'm the cream of the crop. The cherry on the sundae."

"The what?" Firestar's brows scrunched together.

"Never mind." I waved him off. I sometimes forgot that most people in Waesigar had never heard of ice cream. Let alone human sayings in general. I'd have to be more careful on the references in the future.

"Anyway, what I'm trying to say is some things just take time to adjust to. This is one of them.

Even when I'm swollen with child, I will still need to be reminded that I'm desirable. Probably even more so." I twisted my lips at the imagery of my stomach expanding out over my toes. I couldn't say I was looking forward to that part of the pregnancy process.

"You'll always be beautiful to me." Firestar placed his hands on my hips and drew me close to him. I wrapped my arms around his waist as his body heat warmed my own. I wanted nothing more than to curl up in his embrace and forget about everything else.

Nevertheless, I couldn't. There was still his father to deal with, and Raiden and Jack were waiting for me. I couldn't leave them now any more than I could have back in the bathroom of Lord Amun's palace.

"What are we going to do?" I muttered against his chest allowing myself a few moments of comfort.

"Well, first off," Firestar leaned away from me to look at my face. "We are going to find you somewhere to sleep for the night."

I opened my mouth to interject.

"And your dragon concubines."

Shoving at his shoulder, I frowned even as the

smile threatened to come forward. "They aren't concubines."

"I know," Firestar smirked. "But it's so much fun to tease you. In fact," he sidled up next to me once more his hands gripping my waist bringing me flush against his front, "I remember you used to like being teased."

"That was before." I placed my hands on his arms, trying to extricate myself from him. We were too close, and I didn't trust myself to be this close to him and not give in.

"What does that matter?" Firestar wouldn't budge.

"We can't do this, Firestar," I growled out in frustration.

"Why not?" One of his hands slid down to cup my backside and press me firmly against the hardness inside his pants. I forced back a groan as I fought against my own body's reaction. Desire pulsated through my very being begging for a reprieve, but Firestar wasn't done with me yet. He tangled his fingers in my hair and drew my head to the side where his mouth attacked my neck and ear. A whimper fell from my lips, and for the life of me, I couldn't find the will to push him away.

When his tongue found the spot behind my ear,

my legs crumbled beneath me, leaving Firestar's arm to hold me up. My hands clutched at his shirt, holding on for dear life as he used his wicked mouth on me to disperse any neurons in my brain while the hand gripping my butt slid between my legs stroked at my heat. My legs quaked as my thighs slickened, and before I knew it, Firestar had me up and over the edge.

Moments after I cried out my release, reality set in. I shoved him away from me. This time he let me, an arrogant grin on his face. "You shouldn't have done that," I snapped.

"I'll ask again, why not?" His eyes were dark with lust and his voice deep, it made my core ache to be touched again.

"Because I'm not here for that," I argued, holding a finger up to hold him off. "I came with Raiden and Jack and I can't… we can't." I stumbled over my words for a moment and then stopped. I took a deep breath in and let it out, centering myself. "I promised nothing would happen, and I will not break my promise. I already lied about us knowing each other. I won't make things worse."

Firestar stopped coming toward me and frowned. "You're serious."

"Yes." I threw my hands up in the air. "Finally, you get it. This…" I gestured between us, "we can't happen. No matter what your father has done or will do. I'm here for the treaty, and that's it."

The fire dragon was quiet for a moment and then straightened his back and nodded. "Very well. I will have Blorder escort you to your living quarters."

"What about your father?" I asked, moving toward the tent flap.

"Tomorrow we will discuss what to do about my father and all that entails. Now go." He waved me away, his eyes turning back to the table where we had once sat "Before I change my mind."

I hurried out of the tent not because I thought he would force me to do anything I didn't want to do, but because I knew my restraint had already taken all it could bear. I didn't trust myself not to give in to him if he seriously tried to get me in bed. Now I just needed a cold shower to remind my body of that.

15

Blorder didn't like me. I could tell by the way he kept shooting daggers my way when he thought I wasn't looking. Or the way he dropped me off at a tent without a word before stomping away.

Sighing, I stared at the tent in front of me. It looked exactly like all the others, meaning someone probably got kicked out so we could have it. No wonder Blorder didn't like me.

As I stared at the entrance, I wondered briefly if Raiden and Jack were in there, but a cough from inside answered that question for me. What would I tell them? They would definitely want to know what happened.

I glanced back at the large tent I had come

from. Firestar was still in there. Was he thinking about me? On the other hand, had he brushed me off after my many rejections? My head told me it was for the best, but my heart thought otherwise.

"Are you going to stand there all night?" Raiden growled from inside the tent. Someone obviously was still mad.

Pulling up my metaphorical big girl pants, I stepped into the tent to face the music.

What lay before me though was not a tent full of angry men but shirtless ones laying out on a large pile of blankets. I'd seen Raiden partially nude but never like this. The tanned skin over ripped muscles combined with the way he was looking at me — as if he remembered how I tasted and wanted more — if my body wasn't already still trembling from Firestar's touch it would be now.

Then they just had to put Jack in the mix.

The stoic man was a sight all of his own. A complete contrast to Raiden, his pale skin almost glowed in the light of the lamp. He had spread his long hair out over his shoulder so that it brushed along the edges of his pants bringing my attention to the faint trail of hair leading down. I licked my lips to wet my suddenly dry mouth. They certainly were a sight to see.

"Maya," the way Jack said my name was like a caress in the most intimate of places. "Why don't you come down here and make yourself comfortable?"

"Yes, come join us." Raiden held a hand out to me. The fun-loving guy I was used to had left and the commanding man who had brought me so much pleasure had taken his place.

While nearly everything in me wanted to eagerly join them, a nagging part of me kept me from doing so. Pushing back my desire, my brows furrowed as I suspiciously tried to figure them out. I had expected to be fighting with them until we all went to bed angry and dissatisfied, but it seemed they had other ideas.

"What's going on here?" I squeaked, partially ashamed I could barely form the words.

Jack and Raiden's faces dropped at my question moments before a scowl replaced Raiden's bedroom eyes and Jack's mask of indifference came back up.

"I told you it would not work," Jack sighed and reached for his shirt. I'd been so surprised by their little setup, I probably hadn't reacted well. They had gone to all this trouble after all.

"Oh, don't get dressed on my account." I reached a hand out to stop him from pulling the shirt over his head, bringing me down to my knees and awfully close to him. "I mean, uh… you were going to bed soon, anyway. Right?"

My thin excuse made Jack's gaze soften, and he dropped the shirt back down on the ground. "If it pleases you to look, then by all means."

My face heated at his words and I turned my attention to the platter of food between them. There was some kind of meat, but it was mostly fruits and vegetables. Reaching a hand out, I picked up an orange slice and brought it to my lips. Taking a bite of it, the juice spurted out dripping down my chin. I started to wipe it away, but a hand stopped me.

My eyes met Jack's as he leaned forward and licked the liquid from my skin. When he didn't immediately retreat afterward, my eyes darted to Raiden. He watched Jack and me with a narrowed gaze as if he didn't trust me not to stab Jack in the back. I understood his distrust. I hadn't been honest about Firestar, and it seemed like it had hurt Raiden the most. Surprising really, since Jack had portrayed himself to be the jealous one. I didn't think I had to worry about Raiden. Apparently, I was wrong.

I shot him a look, challenging him to say something but was distracted when Jack took my lips with his own. Not closing my eyes, I moved my mouth along with Jack's and let him pull me into his lap. A hardness pressed against my backside, and I couldn't help but wiggle my bottom against it. My movement caused Jack to groan into my mouth. My eyes fluttered closed, no longer caring what Raiden thought. I shifted until I could straddle Jack's lap pressing him against my throbbing core.

Needing to breathe, I let go of his mouth and said, "I thought you didn't want an audience?"

"Let's just say, Raiden and I have come to an agreement." His eyes darted behind me before returning to my face. "Does it bother you?"

"No. Maybe. I don't know." I shook my head and sighed. "It's all kind of weird and sudden. What changed?"

"Isn't it obvious?" Raiden snapped from behind me. "He has already started to turn her against us."

Twisting around in Jack's lap, I stared at him. "What are you going on about?"

"You," Raiden sneered. "You hid him from us. You only agreed to do the lord's bidding because you hoped to see him again. Didn't you?"

I shook my head, anger filling me. "No, I didn't."

"Then why didn't you just tell us if you weren't

planning on picking him?" The accusation in Raiden's voice caused a mixture of hurt and shame to swirl inside of me. I had wanted to see Firestar but not to leave them for him. Quite the opposite really.

"Not to be difficult." Jack's hands tightened at my waist, turning my attention back to him. "But Raiden does have a point. Why exactly did you say yes to Lord Amun's request?"

"I admit, I did want to see Firestar but not for the reasons you think," I added before Raiden could jump in. The mood ruined, I slid from Jack's lap and wrapped my arms around my knees before placing my chin on top of them. "Firestar and I were lovers but not just that, he was my first."

"Your first?" Raiden's eyes widened. "Like first kiss, first lover?"

"First everything."

Jack and Raiden were quiet for a moment, and then Jack's hand stroked my hair. "One's first love is an important person and is hard to forget."

"Yeah," Raiden jumped in, offering me a small smile. "You should have told us. We would have understood. Do you think there wasn't anyone before you?"

"I'm not so arrogant." I snorted lifting my head

slightly, not completely sure they would have understood. In my experience men didn't like to talk about one's feelings. Especially, dragons.

"Well, that's something at least." Raiden moved closer, taking a piece of meat from the platter. Somehow, that one movement seemed to lessen the tension in the room, and we spent the next half hour eating and discussing what I had learned from Firestar.

"It is quite a story to swallow," Jack commented after I had finished. "Though, I can't say I am surprised. The palace was too empty to just be a guard against thieves."

"Exactly," I nodded. "I think Firestar is telling the truth, but unless we can get him to come back with us, I don't see how we can fix any of this. I can only see civil war in their future."

"Well, there's nothing we can do tonight." Raiden stretched and yawned. "I don't know about you, but I'm exhausted."

I couldn't have agreed more. I'd been on an emotional rollercoaster since I had heard about Firestar, and I wanted nothing more than to collapse into a blissful sleep. Somehow, I doubted that would come easily.

We settled down onto the makeshift bed, and

someone turned off the lamp, putting us into darkness. I tried to go to sleep, I really did, but something was still bothering me. Something I needed to get off my chest.

"Raiden? Jack?"

"Yes?" Jack answered, and Raiden made a noise telling me he heard me.

"I'm sorry. You know, for not telling you." My hands tightened into fists on the blanket beneath us as I waited for their response. After a moment, they clasped my fisted hands into theirs, and that was how we fell asleep, hand in hand.

16

The next morning, I sought out Firestar to get things going. I didn't want to stay here much longer than I had to, and if his father really was the bad guy, I doubted he'd wait too much longer for us to return with our answer.

When I arrived at his tent, Blorder stood outside the tent flap. Great. How to get around the bodyguard? Blorder's eyes narrowed when they landed on me, and the arms he had crossed over his chest tightened. That wasn't good.

"Hey, Blorder," I tried for a sweet smile. "How are things?"

"Get lost."

My lips pressed into a thin line, my eyes narrowing to match his. "I need to talk to Firestar."

"That's Lord Firestar to you, woman," Blorder sneered.

Placing my hand on my hip, I shoved a finger at Blorder's chest. "I'll call Firestar whatever I damned well please. He's no better than me."

Blorder's eyes flickered behind me and then his expression changed to disgust. "He will always be better than some royal whore."

I glanced behind me to see Jack and Raiden standing by our tent. I'd left them there sleeping while I went to talk to Firestar. I'd hoped not to have to fight today, but Blorder seemed determined to piss me off.

"I suggest you focus on the men you have and stop trying to hook your claws into our lord." Blorder jerked his head toward the guys before dismissing me with a turn of his head.

Growling low, I bared my teeth. "Not that it's any of your business, but I am trying to provide an heir for my kingdom. What have you ever sacrificed for your lord?"

Blorder glared at me. "My wife and child."

My mouth dropped open and then I promptly snapped it shut. After a moment of silence, I crossed my arms over my chest and said, "Look, I'm sorry about your family, but you have to understand something. Firestar and I aren't anything. I'm not trying to seduce him or add him to my group. I just want him and his father to get together so I can get this damned treaty signed. So, will you please… please just let me talk to him?"

The guard's face morphed from anger to delight as he informed me, "He's not here."

Anger rushed through me and before I knew it, I had Blorder by the collar of his shirt and was screaming in his face, "Why didn't you say that in the first place?"

"Get off me, woman!" His hands grabbed at me, trying to shove me off, but I held on tight. I was tired of being the butt of everyone's joke. I didn't want any of this. I didn't ask to have my whole world turned upside down so I could be someone's brood mare. I hadn't sacrificed everything for my kingdom just so this guy could screw with me?

Not on my watch.

Just as I used my magic to search around the earth for something to strangle this idiot with, two sets of hands grabbed me. I clawed out, my hands catching air as the hands pulled me away from Blorder.

"No, let me go." I struggled against them. My fist shot out, and there was a satisfying smack. The grunt that came out sounded like Raiden, but I couldn't be certain because my attention was focused on escaping from them so I could clobber Blorder. My eyes stayed on Blorder who had a shit-eating grin I wanted to rip off his face.

Eventually, Blorder went into Firestar's tent, laughing the whole way and then I couldn't even see it as the hands holding me back shoved me into a tent. My back hit a familiar makeshift bed as Raiden's and Jack's faces appeared above me. My seething cooled a bit, and I closed my eyes with a deep breath.

Letting the breath out, I opened my eyes.

"Better?" Raiden asked with a grin.

I sighed. "You can let me go now, I'm fine."

"Are you sure?" Jack asked, exchanging a look with Raiden. "We do not wish you to come to any harm."

"Yeah, I'm sure." My eyes slid over to Raiden's face where a bruise began to form. "Sorry about that."

Raiden smirked and rubbed the side of his face. "Don't worry about it. It was a love tap."

"Ha. Hardly," I scoffed.

Since Raiden had all but let me go, Jack also released me. I sat up and crossed my legs, I glared at the ground. "I don't know what came over me. I went to look for Firestar so we could discuss what to do, but that jerk wouldn't let me by, and I just snapped." I ran a hand over my face and groaned. "I must have looked like an idiot."

"Never." Jack placed a hand on my shoulder with a gentle crinkle of his eyes.

"You're just saying that to be nice." I pouted. "But thank you."

"Since we are no longer trying to restrain you," Jack glanced to Raiden briefly. "What did the man say to upset you so?"

"Nothing really," I huffed. "He just forgot to mention Firestar had left before I stood there like a fool begging him to let me by."

"Firestar's gone?" Raiden's brow shot up to his hairline. "Where did he go?"

"Beats me." I shrugged and stood from the tent floor causing Raiden and Jack to stand as well.

"He didn't mention anything to you about leaving last night?" Jack lifted the flap of the tent open, allowing me to go first before he and Raiden followed after. My eyes went to the main tent. Blorder still hadn't come back out, or if he did, it had been while we were in our tent. However, I didn't really care about Blorder's whereabouts. I wanted to know where the hell Firestar had gone.

"No. He didn't say anything about leaving." I shook my head, a bit peeved Firestar had taken the time to stick his tongue down my throat but not to tell me his plans when we had an appointment today. I didn't have time to be waiting around for him to show up. I also didn't want to spend too much time with a bunch of would-be bandits who obviously didn't respect any authority other than Firestar.

"What are we going to do?" Raiden asked, his attention on the fighting arena across the camp. "Are we going to wait for him? Or go back to Lord Amun and tell him to shove it?"

"I wish it were that simple, but knowing my father if we come back without the treaty signed none of us will be getting any dessert."

"Is that some kind of Earth analogy?" Jack asked from my side, his face scrunched up in confusion. I kept forgetting myself, letting little things from Earth creep in. I'd only been there five years. You'd think it wouldn't have such an impact on me, but then again, I would kill for some rocky road ice cream right now.

"Yeah, it is." I left it at that and started for the fighting arena. If we were going to be stuck there waiting until Mister High and Mighty decided to grace us with his presence we might as well get some training in.

17

Firestar didn't return until the sky had turned a dark pink, and my patience had reached its breaking point.

I tapped on Raiden's arm and pointed toward Firestar's tent, letting him know I was heading over there. He nodded before turning his attention back to the arena where Jack fought against three different guys at once. I smiled at how easily they had proven themselves to the bandits. Raiden and Jack had not only demolished every single opponent, but now the men were taking bets on the fights. I had no doubt they'd be fine. Me? Not so much.

I tried to keep my rage at a low simmer as I made my way to Firestar's tent. Thankfully, Blorder wasn't guarding the door, so there wouldn't be any repeats of my humiliation. Now, if I could just keep my head enough to figure this whole thing out before I ripped Firestar's off.

All my plans to keep my temper flew out the window when I spot Firestar sprawled out on his bed mat snoring like a... well... dragon!

Stomping across the room, I grabbed the pitcher sitting on the table and dumped it over his head. Firestar jerked awake, his hands went up into a fist, his eyes wide as they darted around the room. When his eyes landed on me, they narrowed, and before I could react, his hand shot out and grabbed me, pulling me down onto the bed mat.

"What do you think you are doing? Let me go." I growled, shoving against his lean, bare chest.

"What was I doing? What were you thinking?" He frowned. "You should know better than to wake up a dragon like that." His hands pinned me to the bed, the heat of his body warming mine in a delectable way, and I had to force back the moan threatening to escape.

I shook the feeling off and glared at him. "Well, I wouldn't have to wake you up if you weren't sleeping when you should be discussing our next move."

Firestar's lips quirked up at the edges. "I know what my next move will be." His hands slid down my arms and settled right below my breasts. The need to arch into his hand needled at me, but as his fingers brushed the underside of my aching chest, I shoved his chest and jumped off the mat.

"You know that wasn't what I meant." I pointed a finger in his direction as I backed away from Firestar and his wandering hands.

"I know." He nodded slightly and then smirked. "You can't blame me for trying."

"Yes, I can." Crossing my hands over my chest, I stared him down.

Firestar stood from the mat and grabbed his shirt from the floor. Dragging it over his head, I watched sadly as his magnificent body disappeared from view. When it was gone, I remembered why I was there in the first place.

"Where have you been this whole time?" I snapped, irritated at my lack of self-control.

"I had an errand to run." His answer only angered me more.

"And you just thought I'd hang around and wait for you to come back?" My hands waved in the air. "I'm not here on holiday!"

Firestar wiggled a finger in his ear, wincing. "I

didn't think you were, and I wasn't exactly messing around all day."

"Oh, really?" I placed my hands on my hips, leaning forward slightly. I didn't believe him for one minute.

"Really." He offered me a genuine smile, but I only frowned.

"Then, where were you?"

Firestar sighed and headed for the table where a plate of cold food waited. "What happened to you? You never used to be this suspicious."

My eyes narrowed at his statement. "Experience."

When your family suddenly turns on you, it wasn't unreasonable to expect your trust level to be virtually nonexistent. It took months before I could really trust Ryan and Bianca, and even then, I never trusted them completely. Otherwise, I'd have told them Waesigar was real, and I was, in fact, a dragon myself. As it were, I only had a limited amount of trust left, and none of it told me Firestar wouldn't pull a fast one over me if I let him.

"Well, your experience sucks." The dragon in question pointed out as he stuffed a hunk of bread into his face. "For your information, I was meeting with my father."

"Your father!" I sat down at the table across from him surprised at his words. "What were you doing there? I thought you said you were banished." My suspicion started to rear its ugly head again.

"Now, hold on a minute." He held his hand up between us. "Don't go jumping to conclusions."

"Then enlighten me." Impatience filled me as he tried to appease me.

"I went to speak to my father about what we talked about. He needs to come clean to the people and stop stealing from them."

"What did he say?" I sat on the edge of my seat, hoping the words he would say next would make everything easier.

"Well, he said no, as I thought he would."

My hopes sank, and I flopped back in my seat.

"But!" Firestar held a finger up. "I mentioned to him, an alternate solution."

"Oh, really?" I raised a brow. "And what exactly would this alternate solution look like?"

Firestar smiled.

"What?" I asked again, that ugly head wiggly up again.

Firestar's grin widened.

"Seriously, Firestar what's going on?" My frown couldn't get any deeper, nor my anxiety any higher.

"You," he said, getting to his feet. He walked the short distance around the table and stood before me. Hand out to me, I hesitated before taking it. He drew me to him, my hands landing on his chest. Firestar cupped my face, and for a moment, it was like we were back in my father's palace. I was that young, naive girl who had butterflies in her stomach because the guy she liked was about to kiss her.

"What about me?" My voice came out a low murmur, and my eyelids fluttered.

"If we became mated, you could help my father pay back his debts."

My eyes snapped open as those butterflies promptly died. "What?"

Firestar smiled fondly down at me. "We can be together like we always wanted."

While his words were tempting. I couldn't forget about the men I came here with. My body and heart wanted him, wanted all that he promised. But two men were waiting for me outside this tent.

"No, we can't."

His expression wilted, and confusion took its place. "Why not? I thought you would be happy."

Pushing away from him, I wrapped my arms

around my stomach as nausea set in. I had wanted to be with him, and a part of me still wanted to but not like this. And not now. There were too many other factors to consider. Others who would get hurt. Raiden and Jack's faces blinded my vision, and I had to shake my head to clear it.

"No."

"What do you mean no?" Firestar tried to pull me back into his embrace, but I held my hands up, standing my ground. Before I could answer, Firestar's eyes narrowed, and his lips curled down. "This is because of them, isn't it?"

"What if it is?" I snapped, throwing my hands in the air. "You can't just assume I would drop them because you said so."

"But what about us?" he asked, his tone dangerous. "Don't we matter anymore? Or are you telling me you don't feel the connection I feel?"

"I do, but it's not that simple. There are other people involved. Don't forget this is all to get an heir for my father." I pleaded for him to understand.

"So, we give him one." Firestar came up to me, placing his hands on my waist. "We can help each other. If we mate, your father's money will help my kingdom, and we have a baby, and that helps your father. It's a win-win."

I pushed his hands away with a sigh. "You still don't get it. I cannot just have a baby with you! The competition is already in play. There are two men out there who have dropped everything just for the chance to be with me, and I can't just send them away to be with you."

"And what? You don't think I would drop everything too?" His eyebrows rose, and incredulous look came over his face.

A flashback of how I'd found out he'd left filled my mind. Shaking my head, I turned away from him. "You didn't do it back then. Why would you do it now?"

"Is that what it takes?" Firestar's hands landed on my shoulders. When I didn't respond, his grip tightened. "Fine. I accept." He released me with a sigh.

"What?" I turned around my face scrunched up in confusion. "What do you accept?"

"I'll be part of your little competition."

"No," I said so shocked I could barely breathe. "That's not what I said at all."

"Then what?" he practically shouted anger coloring his face. "I don't have a chance with you unless I play your game. So, consider myself in the running and believe me when I say, I won't be losing." Firestar pulled me toward him, his hand tangling in my hair as his mouth crashed down on mine. All my repressed emotions rushed through me, and I wanted nothing more than to sink into his embrace.

I didn't struggle against him, too surprised to even know where to start. Then when his hands moved beneath my top, I ripped my mouth from his, doubt suddenly surfacing. "Wait, wait." I breathed my chest heaving.

"No, no more waiting. I've waited long enough to be with you again, and this time I'm not letting you go." The beast inside of him caused his voice to come out a low growl, and my dragon resonated in response. She'd missed him and his dragon. Not that I could blame her, but it had taken all I had to fight against the pull Firestar had on me before. Now that our beasts wanted to play, keeping a hold on my need was virtually impossible.

And the thing was, I didn't want to fight it. Not really, not anymore, and not with him. What I wanted, more than anything, was to give in.

"All right," I murmured below lowered lashes

"All right?" Firestar brushed my hair away from my face his own eyes going soft.

Was this a good idea? Probably not. Would it

come back to bite me in the butt? Most likely. But could I find a good enough reason to tell him no? Could my heart tell him no? Not when Firestar looked at me like that, as if he wanted to devour me whole, leaving no part of me untouched.

My beast and I agreed for once. Even if Firestar didn't end up being the one I picked, I owed it to my younger self to try, to see if we could be something. To get what we never could before. I'd also be lying if it didn't admit I wanted him probably just as much, if not more, now than I did the first time around.

I licked my lips and swallowed hard as I said the words which would either save or condemn us, "All right, you can be in the competition."

"Good." The single word set my body on fire as he captured my mouth with his once more. His hand angling my head just so to drive me into oblivion. I gripped his shirt in my hands until it balled up, pressing up on my tiptoes to get as close to him as possible.

Pulling on his shirt, Firestar released my mouth long enough for me to remove it, and then his lips attacked once more. He was everywhere. On my mouth, on my neck, and when my shirt came off, his tongue and mouth were teasing and sucking on my breasts. I gasped and arched my back as his teeth scraped against my nipples before Firestar moved on from my chest.

Hands tangled in his head of flaming hair, the background noise of the camp drowned out beneath the rush of heat in my veins. Each lick of his tongue along my skin caused my body to ignite, and I feared before we were done, the flame would consume me.

Too caught up in the feelings Firestar had created, I didn't even realize we had moved to the mat on the floor until my hands reached out and grabbed the blankets beneath me. My pants had been removed at some point baring me to the cool air of the room. Soon the cold wasn't a problem anymore because Firestar was there, quickly driving me higher and higher. We weren't even having sex yet, and already I felt close to exploding.

"God, I've missed you," Firestar growled against my skin as he breathed between my thighs. "I've missed this." His fingers stroked along my folds, causing me to groan as pressure built inside of me. My eyes rolled to the back of my head as Firestar quickly brought me to my release. He still knew just how to play my body, and with my luck, my heart wouldn't be too far behind.

He moved back up my body until his eyes locked with mine. The desire there matched my own, and I knew I wasn't the only one who had craved this. I wasn't the only one who wanted to pick up where we left off all those years ago, before my father broke us up. Now we had that chance.

When he slipped inside of me, nothing mattered anymore. Not my father or the mission he had given me. All that mattered was the press of his body against mine, the pleasure that rippled through me with each stroke as we reached for our release. My hands grabbed at him, nails biting into his shoulders. When he hit a spot deep inside of me, causing me to cry out, the scent of blood tinged the air from where I held onto him, afraid I would fall apart if I didn't have something to hold me together.

"That's it, Maya," Firestar growled in my ear his body still thrusting against mine, forcing me to climb to my release again and again. Each one more intense than the last as they left me gasping for breath and begging for relief. But it was in vain. Once Firestar started, he wouldn't stop until my legs became jelly and nothing but him filled my very soul. It was that very aspect of him I fell in love with, and the one which made me hold onto him tighter as he finally found his own pleasure.

He rolled off me, so as not to crush me, and chuckled.

"What?" I asked between deep breaths. I had forgotten how much being with him took out of me, and I wasn't even doing most of the work!

"I knew it could be like it was before." Those were the only words he said before he started to snore. I rolled my eyes, too tired to gripe at him about it.

As I lay next to him on the mat, I briefly wondered how I would explain it to Jack and Raiden. They had been so understanding and willing to share me, I had a hard time thinking they would object. Looking down at the dragon beside me, I didn't know if my heart would even let me if they did. I knew my inner dragoness wouldn't, and that spelled trouble for everyone.

18

I shifted on the mat only half awake, still caught in some dream about Waesigar 2 and three avatars which looked vaguely like the three dragons who were vying for my hand. Or rather my child.

It only became worse when my senses started to awaken, and my nose filled with the scent of Firestar, and what we had done last night. My body heated in remembrance and a certain part of me tingled for more. Then I turned over on the mat, my hand reaching out for an encore only to come up empty.

Sitting up, I searched the dimly lit tent. Firestar had been there with me when I fell asleep, but he wasn't now. No one was.

I flopped back down on the mat and sighed. I shouldn't be surprised. Firestar had never been the kind for cuddling afterward or lazy morning lovemaking. Quick bursts of passion were more his style.

Like you're complaining? A saucy part of me taunted.

While Firestar might be an explosion of pleasure, I couldn't help but think of Raiden. The lightning dragon had alpha male written all over his body. Every delicious inch of it. It made me wonder what kind of lover Jack would be?

Would he be aggressive, like Raiden? Passionate like Firestar? Or would he something completely different?

From the way he kissed me the first time, I'd say he didn't have a lot of experience with women. Or at least, not much. But while our first kiss had been hesitant and unsure, Jack sure had made up for it when we had our little impromptu date. The kiss between us at the end had more feeling than I had seen on his ice sculpture of a face, ever.

I didn't know how to even begin to explain what happened with Raiden and Jack the other night. Jack seemed to have no problem getting in the mood with Raiden there to urge him on. Was Jack secretly an exhibitionist? Raiden seemed to be. Maybe that's why both of them had bonded? Their mutual love for being watched.

A shiver ran through me at the thought. Their preferences were rubbing off on me, and I couldn't find a reason to care. A part of me was intrigued to see how far they would go. And now that Firestar had joined our little group — not that they knew about it yet — I wondered if they would want to share me all around. Now that was a thought.

I climbed out of bed and pulled my clothes on. I needed to find out what would happen next.

Before I could push through the tent flap, Jack came through, making me take a step backward. My eyes lit up at the sight of him, but when I saw the rage in his eyes, my feet scrambled back a few steps until they hit the pole in the middle of the tent.

"Jack, what's going on?" I sputtered, holding onto the pole like it could protect me from his rage.

Jack's eyes darted away from me and to the mat on the floor. His nostrils flared, and he inhaled before letting it out in a violent huff.

"So, it's true."

It wasn't a question, and I didn't bother denying it. It would only make us both look like fools. But I did take the chance to stand behind the pole, creating a buffer between me and the oncoming storm that was Jack. I didn't blame him for his anger. Part of me felt guilty for letting something happen between Firestar and I before I had a chance to talk to them. I didn't bother trying to lie about what happened. It'd only make things worse.

"You don't deny it?" His words had a disbelieving hint to it.

"I'm guessing you aren't too happy about it." So much for my fantasy of all three of them taking me together. Jack's reaction was all wrong. Of course, I had planned on telling him myself and not having him walk into our aftermath.

"When were you going to tell us?" Jack stalked toward me a low rumble in this voice. "Did you think Raiden and I would just step aside so you could ride into the sunset with this man?" He gestured around the room wildly, a move so unlike the usually composed dragon.

"No! No." My placating tone quickly changing to hysterical denial. I sighed and smacked my face with the palm of my hand. "I mean, that's not what I had planned at all. I wasn't going to push you and Raiden aside."

"Then what was your plan?" Jack crossed his

arms over his chest his face a mask of cool indifference. "You thought you could sleep with your ex-lover and Raiden and I wouldn't care?"

"Of course not." I tried to explain further, but he kept going.

"You already slept with one of us, why not add another one to the mix?" He landed in front of me his gaze locked with mine, a thickness filling the air. "Dragonesses do have a hard time getting pregnant, better to have any many chances as possible, right?"

"Right!" I cried out and then shook my head. "I mean, no."

"It sure seems like it from where I am standing." He moved a bit closer until only the pole stood between us, until I could feel his breath on my face. "Believe me, I am looking very hard to find the bigger picture, Maya. But from what I have witnessed, you are in over your head. You don't know what you are getting into."

"I know exactly what I'm getting into," I snapped, the dragon in me roared for a fight. "Then why don't you enlighten me? Help me understand." The challenge in his voice made me frown. It was like he wanted me to admit I was only looking for an excuse to have sex with Firestar.

"Firestar went to see his father yesterday." As I

spoke, my eyes roamed over Jack's face, taking in every angry line.

"I hope you let him know how we felt being left to fend for ourselves." Jack placed his hands behind his back with a frown.

I cocked a brow. "I think we did well to entertain ourselves. I didn't see you complaining."

"And what would that have accomplished?" Jack raised a brow in return.

Sometimes Jack's reasonableness drove me insane. Why couldn't he be like everyone else and kick and scream when something didn't go his way? Instead, he hid behind his mask, pretending everything was okay until it became too much. I wondered if eventually hiding all those emotions would catch up with him. It couldn't be healthy.

"Nevertheless," I sighed. "If it will make you feel better, I did get onto Firestar for abandoning us without a word."

"Was that before or after you mated with him?" The bite in Jack's voice made me wince. I guess he didn't really hide his emotions as well as he thought.

"Before," I gritted my teeth.

At this rate, it would take forever to get through what happened. Sadly, I didn't think it would make Jack feel any better about my sleeping with Firestar.

He might not act like it, but he probably still had a thorn in his side about me choosing Raiden first. He seemed like the type who didn't want to be the second choice. His decision to share me at all was surprising at best.

"Then what? Was your mating just a convolution of emotions running high and seeing your first love after so long? Or something else?" He leaned against the pole, and I stepped back to give us some space. Only one of us needed to be distracted by our feelings right now.

"Neither actually." I walked away from Jack and moved over to the table. I sniffed the pitcher sitting there and grimaced as the sharp sting of Dragon's Tears hit my nose. Did Firestar drink anything else? Either way, my mouth felt as dry as a bone and the way our conversation was headed, a drink was needed.

I poured a glass and took a large drink of it before setting it back down on the table. I turned around and leaned back against the edge with my hands, bracing myself as I stared down at the ground.

"Firestar thinks if he becomes my mate, my father will help him pay off his father's debts."

"Hmm." Jack rubbed his chin. "That will end

the attacks on the people and allow Firestar to return home."

"Exactly." I glanced up from the ground to meet his gaze. His eyes weren't angry anymore, but there was still a bit of torment there, meaning my work wasn't done yet.

"So, anyways. He wanted us to pick up where we left off, you know before I was banished." I gestured in the air. "But I told him I couldn't do that."

"Why ever not?" Jack seemed surprised, and it showed across his normally well-guarded features.

I smiled slightly. "That's what he asked too."

This made Jack frown, and I almost laughed out loud. It was hilarious how much alike they were sometimes. Sadly, I didn't think Jack would appreciate my amusement. Instead, I returned to the topic, no matter how awkward, at hand.

I pressed my lips together tightly before letting them go with a loud pop. Leaving my post, I strolled across the room until I stood before Jack. Placing my hands on his chest, I felt him tense as if he were preparing for an attack. His reaction made my heart ache.

"The reason I couldn't tell Firestar what he wanted to hear was because of you and Raiden." I glanced up at him beneath my lashes, watching his reaction to my admission.

"But why would you do that?" Jack looked down at me, his facade breaking enough for me to see his confusion. "You've only known us for a few days, but Firestar, you've known…"

"Only a few days before we broke up," I interrupted him. "Or rather he took off." I sighed and placed my head on Jack's chest. His heartbeat calmed me slightly, and I let myself settle into the feeling for a moment before I pulled back. "I don't know him any more than I know you and Raiden, and to be honest, I feel like I know you guys much more."

Jack's rubbed my shoulders with slow, soothing motions. "I didn't know."

"How could you?" I met his gaze a bit shyly. "You don't know me that well either. We don't exactly have the time to get to know each other."

"Yes, I suppose not. Your father only wanted us to find physical attraction, not emotional." Jack dropped his hands and brushed his hair over his shoulder, a nervous gesture I'd never noticed before.

"He has his priorities straight, that's for sure." I offered Jack a smile, but when he didn't return it, I frowned.

"You have told me why you didn't accept his proposal, but you haven't told me why you decided to mate with him?" His pale eyes glanced over to the mat, a slight sneer on his face.

"Because..." I trailed off and dropped my arms from Jack, putting some space between us. I wasn't sure how he would react to what I had to tell him. "I might not have agreed to run away with him, but I did agree to allow him to become one of my suitors."

I held my breath as I waited for Jack's reaction. I could imagine he wouldn't be too happy. Who wanted yet another person to compete with for my affections. Or rather my womb.

"So, he would be like Raiden and me?" Jack said slowly as if trying to make sure he hadn't misunderstood me.

"Yes."

"Which is why you mated with him last night?" He locked eyes with me, searching for something in my face. Did he not believe me?

"Yes and no," I admitted. "While he now is part of the competition, a part of me did miss him. I wanted to be with him."

"Then why bother letting him compete? Why not just tell us to leave and focus all your attention on him? It would be faster." His anger was back, and I quickly moved closer to him, not wanting to fight anymore.

"Because it's not just about him. It's about us. I don't know exactly what I feel, but I know I feel something." I cupped his face with my hands. "And I can't just focus all my attention on one of you when my emotions are so scattered between the three of you. What if I pick wrong?"

"What if you don't?" Jack asked, placing his hand on top of mine and squeezing slightly. "What if you and Firestar are meant to be, and we are just standing in your way?"

My eyes pricked with emotion, and I reached up on my tiptoes before pressing my lips to his in a soft kiss. I released him before it could become more. "Believe me, you aren't in my way."

Jack gave me one of his rare smiles. "I'm glad to know it. Now," he drew me away from him keeping my hand in his as he started for the tent flap, "we should probably let Raiden know before he rips Firestar apart."

"What?" I asked, my eyes going wide, and my voice rising in pitch.

Jack paused, and guilt covered his face. "I may have intentionally left out the part where Raiden attacked Firestar, and they are fighting for your hand at this very moment."

"Jack!" I screeched and pushed passed him. I shoved through the tent entrance and into a war zone.

The men of the camp were lined along the edges of the tents, some of the shouting out encouragements, other's insults. A lot of the neatly piled weapons and supplies had been strewn all over the camp, and in the middle of it all, Raiden and Firestar locked in a battle.

Firestar had a cut on his forehead which bled profusely, and the side of Raiden's shirt had a dark patch from where he bled through. At this rate, I wouldn't have to pick between the three of them because Jack would be the only one left.

Anger raged through me, and before I knew it, I was stomping toward the two of them. The men moved parted like the red sea as I surged forward. A low rumble came from my throat as I stopped at the edge of the fight.

"What the hell is going on here?" I shouted, waving my hands above my head, but neither of them paid me any mind. The only thing Firestar and Raiden seemed to care about was beating each other to death.

"Well," Jack came up behind me. "What should we do now?"

"Just let them fight it out," Blorder, who I hadn't noticed beside me, said. "You will see our lord is the far superior choice to be your mate."

"I thought you didn't want me near him?" I glared.

Blorder shrugged, "My lord told us about the deal. If you can help our people, you can't be that bad."

"Well, thanks. I'm so honored," I muttered with a roll of my eyes. I turned to Jack. "Can't you break them up?"

"I can try." He frowned, his eyes following their movements. "But I'm afraid it may turn into two against one, and you may not have any suitors by the end."

Gritting my teeth, I stomped my foot. "Goddammit!" I had to do everything myself.

19

By the time I got up the nerve to step between the two fighting dragons, they had taken to the air. Without wings of my own, I was a sitting duck with nothing left to do but wait for them on the ground.

I almost turned to Jack to ask him to intervene but remembered what he had said. Did I really want to risk the last of my men to break them up? But I also couldn't do nothing, they were fighting for no other reason than because of their male egos.

I stomped over to Blorder and with my hands firmly on my hips, glared. "Can't you make your men stop them?" I gestured angrily toward the fighting dragons.

Blorder crossed his arms and watched the fight

with a bored expression. "Why? He's our lord if he wishes to fight the young one that is his business. What is it to me?"

I scoffed at his nonchalance. Didn't anyone here give a crap about anything other than fighting? No matter what Firestar and I had done together, Blorder clearly still hadn't changed his opinion about me. My helping their people was only a means to an end.

The thought gave me an idea.

I turned to Blorder once more this time trying to appeal to his honor. "You know, I can't help your people if your lord is dead?"

Blorder's face scrunched up as if confused by my words. Then he tightened his stance, not even bothering to look at me as he said, "My lord will not lose."

"Oh, really?" I taunted him. "You are that sure of his powers?"

He nodded, though I could sense a hint of hesitation. Blorder didn't have a hundred percent faith in his lord. He might have seen Raiden fight, but he didn't know for sure Firestar would win, and based on how the fight was going, Firestar might actually be the one to lose.

Focusing my attention back on the battle in

front of us, I watched with growing anxiety as Firestar wavered under Raiden's attacks. Firestar might have had years of fighting on the lightning dragon, but Raiden had the power. Even more so now that he had gained abilities from sleeping with me.

As if knowing my thoughts, Raiden conjured the lightning-powered trident and swung it through the air in one lithe motion. I couldn't tell Firestar's reaction with his back to me, and even though he barely managed to dodge, I had a feeling he wasn't so sure of himself now.

"A little toy like that will not stop Firestar," Blorder said from my side, but I felt like his words were more for his benefit than mine.

I sighed and rocked back on my heels, trying to play it as if I wasn't freaking out. "I don't know. I've seen Raiden take out several powerful fighters at once with that thing, Firestar might be in over his head."

"Then why do you not stop them?" Blorder finally asked with a hint of exasperation. "You claim to love my lord, but you clearly seem in favor of the other dragon. Is your heart so easily swayed?"

My brows furrowed and my jaw clenched. It

was one thing to question my dragon's abilities, it was another altogether to question my heart. I'd had about enough of his mouth.

"Now wait just a minute," I growled and turned my anger onto the guard. "I haven't seen Firestar in years. It is not my fault he can't stay out of a fight for a few hours. In the matter of who had me first, Raiden would be the winner. As for who has my heart, all of them hold a piece of it, and I wouldn't try to even choose between the three of them."

"Then if you will not choose, you better get up there and stop them before they kill each other." Blorder nodded upward where Firestar barely dodged Raiden's trident aimed right for his heart.

My heart pounded in my chest as I watched them lash out at each other. Both of the men were well trained, and I couldn't bet on which one would win, even if I wanted to. The fight could go on for hours, and by the time someone conceded, they would be dead or seriously injured. I didn't want either one. I just wished I could find some way to stop them.

Frustrated at my lack of wings keeping me helpless on the ground, I didn't immediately answer Blorder. He didn't know I couldn't fly, and I wasn't about to tell him. The jerk didn't need another reason to hate me more than he already did. I crossed my arms over my chest and squinted up the in the sky. The sun had risen high enough now that it became hard to make out more than the silhouette of the two.

After a minute or two, the feeling of the fight seemed to change. A charge filled the air, making my hair stand on end. It wasn't coming from Raiden though. The rise in power came from Firestar. The temperature rose until sweat dripped down my face. The fireballs he had been throwing at Raiden hadn't been doing much damage, Raiden having had dodged or knocked them away with his trident.

This time though, it felt different. Firestar held his hands out to each side as magic pulsated from him. Flames burst from his hands, but instead of turning into balls of fire like before, they began to change. The flames lengthened in his grip until they became two kusarigamas, sickle-shaped weapons with long chains used to make attacks from a distance.

Raiden flew back suddenly, barely dodging Firestar's kusarigama as it swung out by the chain. Even still, the flaming weapon almost gutted him. Unfortunately, this didn't make Raiden see reason and forfeit the match. If anything, it made him more determined. His stance shifted, and magic crackled around him as he tried to stay out of range of Firestar's attacks.

"Has he always been able to do that?" I glanced to Blorder, but his eyes were on his lord an expression of wonder covering his face. "I'll take that as a no."

Suddenly, I felt Jack's presence at my back, and I sighed. "Looks like you and Raiden's theory might be right."

"What do you mean?" Jack asked, and I turned to see his eyes on the men above us.

I ran a hand through my hair and groaned. Being able to grant men a power increase by having sex with them wasn't something I wanted to deal with. If it got out that sleeping with me would give dragons extra powers, God only knew what kind of mayhem it would cause. I wouldn't be safe anywhere.

You should just go back to Earth, an inner voice suggested.

I wished I could, but the same reason as before kept me from doing just that. I couldn't leave them. Though I had only known them for a short time, my heart still told me I was where I was supposed to be, and now that I'd slept with two of them, the chances of me being pregnant were higher. I couldn't leave my child without a father, it wouldn't be right.

Either way, now wasn't the time to think about it. Now was the time to stop my men from fighting.

I stepped closer to Jack and said in a low voice. "Firestar was not able to do that before last night."

Jack's face furrowed in confusion, but then his brows rose up on his forehead. "So, you believe him and you..."

"Yes," I hissed, trying to keep him from telling what I was thinking out loud. I especially didn't want Blorder to know, not after his sickening comment when we first met.

"Then we do not have time for this." Jack nodded toward the two still going at it above.

"Exactly." I nodded in return. "Do you think you can...?"

"I think so, but I must be careful. They are both more powerful than I am now." Jack's eyes held a hint of worry but a fierce determination.

I placed my hand on his arm and gave it a squeeze. "I know you can do it."

Jack's eyes briefly met mine. He cupped my cheek with his hand before his wings burst forth from his back, and he took flight. I held my breath as he carefully approached the fighting duo.

They didn't seem to notice Jack at first, but then Raiden's trident almost hit him. Raiden yelled at him something I couldn't make out from the ground, and Jack shook his head and moved to stand between them. Firestar didn't seem bothered by Jack's sudden appearance and prepared to attack again, but before he could, Raiden nodded his head. Then he and Jack descended, leaving Firestar up in the air alone.

As soon as their feet hit the ground, I ran toward them. Jack murmured to Raiden something that caused Raiden's brow to lift and his mouth to turn down in anger. I had a feeling Jack had just told him what we had figured out.

I stopped in front of Raiden, blocking him from going any further. A sudden bout of irritation reared its ugly head, causing my hand to lash out and hit him in the chest. "What the hell do you think you were doing?"

Raiden rubbed the spot I had hit though I knew it hadn't really hurt him. I might be a dragon lord's daughter, but I was still the weaker of the bunch. "You didn't hear what he was saying about you, about us. I couldn't just stand by and let him make a fool of you."

I shook my head and threw my hands up in the air. "I don't know what is worse. Jack's jealousy or your rashness."

"But wait a second—"

"No!" I snapped, cutting him off. "I will not wait a second. We came here to do a job, and I have done it. Without either of your help by the way." I shot a glare at the two. "You seemed too caught up in being the one who ends up with me to even stop to ask me what I want."

"What do you want?" Firestar voice asked from behind me.

I spun around and found the fire dragon standing a few feet away. His wings were still out, and they were as magnificent as they were the first time I saw them. Long and feathered, they burned with a fire which came from within. While most of his kind had wings of fire as well, his had always held a different kind of unearthly beauty to them. Just one more of the things about him I had been drawn to in the first place.

When my eyes finally stopped ogling his wings, they locked onto his gaze, which showed a hint of impatience and anger. I opened my mouth to explain but then remembered the group of onlookers still listening in.

"I want to get out of here is what I want." Before any of them could say another word, I stomped out of the makeshift circle and toward the crowd of men. They parted before me with curious expressions, but I ignored them. I walked past the large tent where I had stayed the night before and kept walking. I didn't stop until I had long since left the camp and found myself surrounded by trees.

Sighing, I plopped down on the ground. I didn't know where I was going or even where I was, but I just needed to get away from them. Ever since I'd been back, I'd be surrounded by people. People who wanted something from me, and I was tired of it. I just needed some room to breathe.

I sat on the ground my knees bent in front of me for what seemed like hours. The quiet of the forest around soothed my frustration and anger enough that I realized I shouldn't have left on my own. Letting out a sigh, I stood to my feet and dusted off myself. I glanced up at the sky and saw the sun had risen to its highest peak.

Must be lunchtime. My stomach rumbled its agreement. Frowning, I searched for the way I'd come and realized I was utterly lost.

"Great," I growled and threw my hands up in the air. "That's what I get for throwing a fit like a child and leaving without a map or provisions. Stuck in the woods by myself."

"Now, I wouldn't say that."

"Raiden. What are you doing here?" I swung around toward the familiar voice and almost collapsed on the ground in relief.

Raiden grinned as he leaned against a tree, amusement clear in his eyes. "Watching you beat yourself up, and you're doing a good job I might add."

Heat filled my face as embarrassment came over me. I crossed my arms and stared down at the ground as I muttered, "Well, can you blame me? I've kind of made a mess of everything."

"No, not really," he answered, coming away from the tree to stand before me. "You weren't the only one who made bad decisions. We were all there to help things along, and like you said, we didn't exactly ask you what you wanted."

"But I shouldn't have just decided like that without consulting you and Jack first," I countered, tucking my hands in my back pockets.

"This is true." Raiden placed his hands on my

shoulders and squeezed lightly. "But this isn't about us, this is about you."

A rustle of brushes jerked my attention from Raiden's comforting words. Firestar came through the trees with a determined look on his face. "And what you might carry inside of you."

"Great." I jerked away from Raiden. "You guys are as bad as my father. The only reason I'm important is because of what I can give you, not because you care about me at all. How do I know once I give birth, you won't be out the door?" My hand swept viciously in the air.

"You don't." I turned at the sound of Jack's voice appearing behind me. "None of us do." His calm gaze fell on me as he approached his hands folded behind his back. "As Raiden said, we have contributed to how things ended up today. Raiden and I have been caught up in our own wants and needs and forgot one important aspect of this trip."

"And what would that be?" I rolled my eyes.

Jack smiled slightly. "You, of course. None of this matters if you aren't here. You could very well return to Earth and leave this behind. Leave us behind."

I shook my head at his suggestion. "I wouldn't do that. Not now that I might be…"

"But you would if you had to," Firestar interrupted. "You think you have changed so much since we last met? But I know you, Maya." His dark eyes locked onto mine pinning me in place. "You are fiercely loyal to the point of insanity, but if someone you loved might be in danger, like your unborn child, you wouldn't hesitate to take off no matter how much it might hurt those around you."

I didn't bother to argue because I knew he was right. If I had to, I would leave. Even if it broke my heart. "So? Why do you care? I'm just a means to an end, right?" I snapped, my hurt turning to anger. "Let's have sex with Maya, she'll give us great powers who cares what she wants. Not that any of you care about me, anyway."

"That's not true, and you know it," Raiden growled true anger in his voice. "Besides being pig-headed jerks have we once said we didn't care for you? That you were nothing but breeding stock?"

I frowned and chewed on my lip before murmuring, "No."

"Then why would you think that now?" Jack came up beside me, placing his hands on my arms. "You have a right to want to be alone, to run away. I can understand how overwhelmed you must be, but running away won't solve anything."

I sighed and leaned into his embrace. "I know. I'm just tired of fighting. Of being a buffer for all of you guys' hang ups. If we have this much of a problem without me being pregnant, what is going to happen when I am?"

Jack brushed the back of my hair with his hand. "Do not worry, Maya. We will be here for you."

"And we'll work on keeping our egos in check," Raiden said from behind me, his front brushing my back. "Besides, one hormone driven crazy female dragon is about all I can handle right now."

I half-laughed through the tears which pricked my eyes. I settled into their embrace, their closeness calming me of my doubts and worries until I realized one person wasn't joining in.

Opening my eyes, I pulled away from Jack to search out Firestar. He stood a few feet away from us, the muscles in his arms bulging as he tightened his arms over his chest.

"And what about you?" I asked, moving closer to him. "Can you be part of the team?"

"What team?" Firestar growled. "I will be the father of your child, why should I play nice with them?"

"Because you might not be, and you have to come to terms with that. Besides, even if you are," I turned to Raiden and Jack. "I don't, no, I won't give them up because you can't share."

"I thought you loved me." His voice was so low and unsure, it hurt my heart.

I placed my hand on his face with a small smile. "I did, and a part of me still does, but it's been a long time, Firestar. Love takes time, and we need time to discover who we both are again, and whether or not we can all be together." I shrugged. "But either way, you're now part of this competition. If you want to win, you'll have to earn it."

Firestar didn't say anything for a moment, and then he dropped his arms pulling me in close. "Fine. For you, I will try anything."

"Good." I smiled and laughed, "Because we haven't even faced the hardest battle yet."

"And what's that?" Firestar asked.

"Telling my father."

20

After our not so mutual agreement, the guys convinced me to go back to Firestar's camp. For some reason, when we arrived, the whole camp went quiet. The men stared at us with a mix of expressions. Some leering, some curious, and others afraid.

"I take it our little secret isn't so secret anymore," I muttered as I moved a bit closer to Jack and Raiden with Firestar leading us through the tents.

"Yeah," Raiden sighed. "Someone must have overheard us and couldn't keep their mouths shut. We'll have to be more careful in the future."

"If I have a future," I shot back. "Maybe we shouldn't have come back."

Jack took my hand, his eyes never leaving the staring crowd. "We didn't have many options. You took off without any provisions, and it's more than a day's hike back to Lord Amun's palace. We had to come back."

"Then maybe I should have waited in the forest while you got supplies." My grip tightened on Jack's hand. The way the men were looking at me was making my skin crawl.

"That might not have been a bad idea," Raiden agreed. The air thickened and lightning crackled along Raiden's hand before his trident formed. He held it firmly in his grip a warning to those who might try to come after me.

"They are loyal to me," Firestar said from the front. "They will not take what is mine."

"Ours," Raiden and Jack said in unison, making me grin slightly. They sure had taken this team thing to heart.

"Anyway," Firestar continued, "I will gather the supplies while you wait in my tent. It will at least stave off some of the attention."

"Fine," I huffed. "Not like we have much of a choice."

When we arrived at the tent, Blorder waited for us, and from the look on his face, he wasn't happy.

"My lord, you've returned and with the woman. Good." He nodded toward me with a different kind of look, one that made me wish he still saw me as a loose woman. Well, he could just go jump off a cliff.

"I am only here to get supplies, and then I will be going with Maya back to my father's and then to the Western Region," Firestar explained, making his guard's expression change. Firestar didn't seem to notice, but I had a bad feeling about it. "I expect you to take charge, and when you have gotten word from me, to return to your homes, peacefully."

"Peacefully?" Blorder exclaimed. "And return home to what? Most of us have left behind our families for your cause, and now you wish us to just go back with nothing to gain for it?"

Firestar seemed to grasp the situation. His eyes narrowed. "You are under my command, and if I tell you to go home, you are to do as I say, not question it."

"And what about her?" Blorder gestured toward me, making Jack take a step in front of me. "Are you to keep her to yourself? Don't think we don't know what caused your little display of power. We aren't fools, Firestar."

Firestar scoffed and then laughed, clearly disgusted. "You think I would just pass her around?" He stepped back from Blorder to look at the rest of his men. "Are you so power hungry, you would take an unwilling woman just to give yourself an advantage?"

The men gave a mixture of responses none of which made me feel any better. I twisted my wrist at my side slowly calling my magic without bringing attention to it. If things were going to get ugly, we would have to be prepared and get out of there fast.

Firestar shook his head sadness on his face. "Then you are not the men who I thought you were."

"And you aren't the leader we thought you were," Blorder jumped in. "We followed you because we thought you were going to make our kingdom great again after your fool of a father put us into debt and stripped our people of what little they had. Now, look at you. You are worse than your father."

Firestar's rage could be felt in the air, and I knew this wouldn't end well even before the kusarigama shot out. It wrapped around Blorder's neck and burned its way through his flesh before he could even let out a scream. Blorder's head fell to the ground and rolled to stop at my feet. My stomach lurched, making me thankful I hadn't eaten yet today.

"Anyone else want to log a grievance?" Firestar shouted, and the crowd stepped back, their initial displeasure overtaken by Firestar's violence.

Firestar's jaw clenched, the kusarigama still in his hand as he said, "Jack, you take Maya inside. Raiden, there is a supply tent right over there." He pointed toward a much smaller tent a few yards away.

"What are you going to do?" I asked as Jack tried to usher me inside. Not that I was fighting him, I'd rather be safely inside than out here any day.

"I'm going to stand guard and make sure no one else gets any ideas." Firestar swung the sickle on its fiery chain, his eyes scanning the dispersing crowd.

"All right," I breathed, trying not to throw up at the head still sitting a few feet away. "Just be careful please?"

"Of course." He smirked and jerked his head to the tent. "Now go."

Jack and I headed inside while Raiden jogged toward the supply tent. Anxiety racked through me as we waited for the all clear. The camp seemed quieter than usual which made me worry things hadn't ended completely. I feared we might not make it out of the camp alive again.

"Do not worry," Jack took my hand and giving it a reassuring squeeze. "Firestar and Raiden know what they are doing. None of us will let them take you."

"I knew this was a bad idea." I stared hard down at the ground, trying to relax but not being able to. "We should have waited where we were and sent them to get stuff. Or maybe even just did without. I'm not a forager, but I'm sure we could have managed."

"But then Firestar would have to come back eventually to send his men home," Jack explained. "Would you want him to abandon them without a word like your father did you?"

I glared at him. "That was a low blow."

"Still," Jack stroked the back of my hand. "You know I am right."

"So, you don't have to be so smug about it." I pulled my hand away from his, enjoying his touch a little too much.

Jack opened his mouth, but the sound of fighting from outside the tent cut off whatever it was he was going to say. Jack and I jumped to our feet as a cry of pain was suddenly cut off.

I started for the tent flap, but Jack stopped me, putting himself in front of me. My lips pressed together in a thin line, the whole damsel in distress thing becoming old, but I didn't object. Whoever came through that flap might very well be there to hurt me.

When Raiden's two-toned hair showed, I couldn't have been more relieved. I rushed to him, wrapping my arms around his waist. The pack on his back got in the way, but I didn't let it stop me.

"What's all this about?" Raiden laughed, putting his arms around me.

"We heard a fight," Jack explained as he approached us. "We feared something might have happened."

Raiden shook his head as he released me. "That was just Firestar taking out another one of his men. I think the rest have decided they would rather go home to their families than risk his blade."

"Good," Jack nodded. "Then we can get going without worry of attack. Come, Maya, stay behind me." He positioned me where he wanted me and turned to Raiden. "You watch our backs."

"Got it." Raiden moved to stand behind me as Jack started toward the tent flap.

I held my breath as he put his hand up in the air behind him, signaling for me to wait. Then after what seemed like forever, he waved me through.

When I exited the tent, the camp was as bustling as ever, but this time it wasn't the usual kind of bustle. There was no joking or playful fighting in the arena. No, everyone moved like they were running late for some big event. When my eyes landed on Firestar, I realized why they were running.

Five bodies littered the ground before him, each of them headless. Very little blood covered the scene because of the fire in his weapon for which my stomach was thankful. The display had a very clear message, mess with him and die. I for one was happy Firestar was on my side.

"So, what now?" I asked as Jack stopped our party next to Firestar.

"We head to my father, and then we go deal with yours." Firestar sighed and looked down at the men at his feet with disgust and a bit of regret. "Did you get what we needed?"

"Yeah, it's all right here." Raiden patted the backpack with a self-satisfied grin.

"Good." Firestar nodded and turned his attention back to the scurrying crowd. "I don't want to stay here any longer than we have to. The sooner we leave, the better."

"Well, you don't have to tell me twice," I started to move away from the bodies and toward the exit. "Let's get out of here."

Before I could get much further, Raiden shouted, "Maya! Watch out."

I threw myself down on the ground just in time for a flying dragon to swoop above me right where I had been standing before.

Firestar's kusarigama hissed by me and wrapped around the dragon. I inched to my knees just in time to see him fighting to pull it off his midsection. Every touch burned him, and Firestar pulled hard on the chain ripping the blade through him, leaving two halves before me.

"Oh my God," I gulped in small gulps of air. "I think I'm going to be sick." Jack came to my side and offered me a hand to my feet. I gratefully took it and held onto him tight. I might be a fighter, but all this killing was playing havoc on my stomach. Suddenly running away to Earth didn't seem like such a bad idea.

"Are you okay?" Jack asked, his arms tightening around me.

"Yeah," I nodded still a bit in shock. "I'm fine. Let's just get out of here."

"Now will you let us fly?" Raiden whined, and this time I didn't argue. My pride didn't matter anymore, my safety did. If I had to suck it up just to get the hell out of there, I would let them fly me all the way home.

"Yes, let's just get out of here."

"Finally!" Raiden cried out in victory and turned to Jack. "You want to take her? Or let..." he trailed off as his eyes turned to Firestar.

Firestar shook his head. "As much as I'd love to, I think it best if I act as guard and ice boy here takes her."

"Ice boy?" I cocked a brow at Jack, who only rolled his eyes. "All right then, ice boy. Looks like you're up."

Jack ignored my teasing and scooped me up, cradling me in his arms. His wings sprouted from his back, and for a moment, I was mesmerized by their beauty.

"God, I hope my wings are that pretty," I murmured to myself.

"I'm sure they will be and more," Jack replied, startling me.

"Did I say that out loud?" I flushed and ducked my head down.

"Don't be embarrassed, it is refreshing to know what you think for once." Jack offered me a small smile. "It gives me a break from trying to guess what is behind that mask you wear."

"Mask?" I scoffed and shook my head. "That's funny coming from you. Besides, I don't know what you mean, I'm an open book."

Raiden came up beside us and snorted. "Hardly. Reading you is as easy as the ancient Draconian text."

"I'm not that bad," I argued, but Firestar jumped in.

"Yes, you are. Now if you don't mind we are drawing attention to ourselves." His eyes went to the staring men.

"Very well." I nodded. "Back to Lord Amun's and then home."

The guys grunted in agreement before Raiden and Firestar released their wings as well. Sadly, before I could take in the sight of all three of them winged and glorious, we took flight, leaving the camp behind.

It wasn't my first time being held while flying, but it had been a while. The feel of the wind on my face and the weightlessness of it all couldn't compare to anything they had on Earth. I had the urge to let go of Jack's neck and let my arms fly freely, but I knew if I did so, it would throw him off balance and might make him drop me. Reluctantly, I tightened my grip on him and just enjoyed the feeling while it lasted.

"You're beautiful," Jack whispered in my ear, jerking my attention to the dragon above me. "And once you are with child, I have no doubt you will be radiant."

My face flushed at his compliments, not used to receiving such attention. I hadn't thought much about what I would look like or feel like when I finally did get pregnant. Pregnant dragons weren't something you ran into every day. Hell, I'd never even met one before.

What would I be getting into? How would my pregnancy be different from the humans I'd seen back on Earth? I suppose I could always ask my mother or even look it up but still, the thought made me nervous. It was one thing to try to get pregnant but a completely different one to actually be pregnant.

"I can feel your heart racing," Jack murmured in my ear. "What are you thinking about?"

I sighed against his chest. "I'm not so sure I'm cut out to be a mother. I can hardly control my own life let alone be responsible for another one."

Jack's arms tightened around me, squeezing me close to him. "You'll be fine."

"But what if—"

"But nothing," he interrupted. "You will do great and don't forget..." His eyes went to the other dragons flying just in front of us. "...You won't be alone."

I sighed, and some of my worries went away. He was right. If and when I got pregnant, I wouldn't have to do it by myself. I would have all of them by my side. Or at least I hoped I would.

21

The flight to Lord Amun was uneventful, and truth be told, I couldn't have wished for better. We'd had too much excitement for one day - for one week, as far as I was concerned.

When we stood before Lord Amun, I let Firestar do most of the talking. He knew his father better than me, and since I was still shaken up by the attacks, I didn't trust I wouldn't burst into tears at any given moment.

"Father," Firestar walked toward his father his arms open wide. Lord Amun embraced his son, clapping him on the back.

"I'm so happy to see you again and with my soon to be daughter-in-law?" Lord Amun's gaze landed on me with a broad smile. "Thank you so much for helping us out with our little..." he coughed and muttered, "...problem."

"Not at all." I waved him off, not wanting to talk more about it than I needed to. I'd never been a good liar, and if Lord Amun kept asking questions, he was bound to figure out our rouse.

"Yes," Mon Liz commented. "It's so good of you to step in like this. Especially since you have your own set of problems to deal with." Her eyes lingered on Raiden and Jack. "How are your fellows taking the news?"

"About what?" I asked feigning innocence. I knew exactly what she wanted me to admit and I wouldn't play her game.

"You know," she moved around the room until she stopped at Jack's side. "That you are tossing them aside like yesterday's dragon to be with your old lover. It must sting a little bit."

Jack kept his eyes forward as he answered, "We understand the obligations Maya had to her prior lover and the needs of a kingdom comes first. What are we if we focus on ourselves and let our allies burn?"

"But still," Mon Liz continued, clearly not taking Jack's answer to heart. "You must care for

Maya Rose deeply to let her go so easily and to someone who wasn't even in the running."

"We do." This time Raiden stepped in. "Which is why we are doing the honorable thing by stepping aside."

Mon Liz opened her mouth to no doubt continue her tirade, but Lord Amun cut in. "Mon Liz, enough."

She snapped her mouth closed, crossing her arms over her chest with a huff. "Can you blame me? I just want to be sure our boy isn't jumping into something that would end up hurting him and the kingdom in the long run."

Lord Amun gave me an apologetic frown. "I'm sorry, she worries. But despite my second's doubts, I know your love is true. At least…" he turned his gaze to Firestar. "…if the way my son talked about you is the same way you feel."

"It is," I said, this time not having to lie.

The lord smiled and nodded. "Then I have nothing to worry about and you," he looked to Mon Liz, "will drop this."

The older woman moved to Lord Amun's side her displeasure on her face more prominent than ever. How she could hate me more now than the last time we saw each other, I could hardly fathom.

Unless.

Maybe because she felt responsible for Firestar? Motherly love? No. She didn't seem the type and the way she openly ogled Firestar's muscles said Mon Liz had had high hopes for her and Firestar in the future. Which meant she had as good a reason as any to hate me.

"Get in line," I muttered under my breath.

Lord Amun's gaze shot to me. "What was that, my dear?"

My face heated in embarrassment. "Nothing, just thinking out loud."

"Well, do share," Mon Liz smiled a bit too brightly. "We'd all love to hear your thoughts on this agreement. Wouldn't we?" She turned to Lord Amun, who nodded.

Great.

I bit my cheek to keep from commenting something rude and pretended to be contrite. "I apologize, I'm afraid I am simply becoming impatient to get home."

"Oh, nothing to apologize for!" Lord Amun grinned at me. "I can imagine you would want to get home to tell your father about all that has happened and perhaps get started on your future?" His eyes slid over to Firestar and then back to me.

"Yes, exactly." I agreed not bothering to mention Firestar might not be my future.

Lord Amun waved me forward to witness his signature on the treaty my father had sent with us and then Firestar signed as a witness and then myself. Jack rolled up the document and tucked it into a watertight cylinder.

"Now," Lord Amun clapped his hands together. "Shall we have dinner to celebrate?"

"No, no." I waved him off. "We really should be getting back. My father isn't a patient man as you know."

Lord Amun frowned, stroking his chin and then sighed. "No, I suppose not. Another time then?"

"Of course," Firestar answered for me, coming to my side. He wrapped his arm around my waist and pulled me close to him. "After everything has been taken care of we will have a grand festival."

"Excellent!" Lord Amun smiled. "Well, I won't keep you any longer. Please take care on your trip home. You are a precious commodity." He eyeballed me, his eyes going down to my stomach before he looked to his son, who nodded.

Just what I needed another guy to think of me as breeding stock. Could my day get any worse?

Oh, yeah, it could. I still had to talk to my

father. He wouldn't be happy in the least about our new addition to his little competition.

Since when do you care what he thinks? A voice in my head hissed.

It had a point, but still, it wasn't going to be pleasant. Hell, I was half tempted to tell Lord Amun I would have dinner after all. Before I could change my mind, Firestar ushered us out of the throne room and then out of the palace.

When we had exited the palace gates, I turned to the men. "So, who is carrying me this time?"

The guys looked between themselves a silent question being asked between them before Firestar stepped forward.

"I think it is best if I carry you home. At least, until we are out of sight of the palace." I cocked a brow at his explanation. "You know since my father thinks that I am the front-runner in your suitors."

"And whose idea was that?" I put my hands on my hips.

Firestar frowned at my question. "You know as well as I, he would not have signed the treaty if he didn't think we were a sure thing. If there was even a hint of a chance I wouldn't get the money we needed, he would have held it hostage until we provided it."

He had a point and a good one at that. The problem was, it was going to come back to bite us in the butt and in a major way. Still, I couldn't let Firestar's problems make me biased in my choice, not that it really was a choice. It was more of a whose little guys could reach the finish line first. I really had no say in it.

At least, not right away.

"Very well." I held my arms up for Firestar to pick me up. When I was settled in his arms, I hollered to the others. "Are you guys ready?"

"Yes," Jack responded on the left.

"All set here," came Raiden's answer from the right.

"Good. Now one more show and then we can finally relax." Even as I said the words, I knew it wouldn't be that easy. Lord Amun might have been easy to fool, but my father wasn't. Neither was my sister or mother, who would bombard me the moment I arrived home. I just hoped we could keep it up until we figured something else out, or I ended up pregnant, whichever came first.

22

"What?" my father's voice reverberated through the palace making my mother and sister wince. To say he was taking the news badly would be an understatement.

Growing up with Lord Dannan, I'd quickly learned his different stages of anger. Anywhere from his irritated tick beneath his left eye to the veins pulsating on his forehead, I knew them all. The stage he was at now went far beyond any I had ever seen before.

My father's face had turned a vibrant purple-red shade as if he were an overripe fruit waiting to burst at any moment.

"I knew I couldn't trust this to you," he sneered,

shoving his nose in my face. "You never thought of what was best for us, your family. Only what you wanted."

"That's hardly the case—" I tried to explain, but he kept going.

"I thought your time on Earth might have helped you get over this hothead." He gestured toward Firestar who had done a good job keeping his mouth shut while my father berated us. Far more than I expected for sure.

"Lord Dannan, if I may," Jack interjected, trying to appease my father. "We did accomplish what you wished. Lord Amun signed the treaty."

"But at what cost?" my father shot back. "My kingdom? My daughter? I would rather go to war than this."

I scoffed, "I didn't know I meant so much to you."

"Maya," my mother cried out in disbelief. "Your father might express himself differently, but he does care for you."

"Well, he has a crappy way of showing it." I crossed my arms over my chest and glared at him. "All he seems to care about is if I can provide an heir for our family."

"And have you?" my father asked his anger receding slightly as hope took its place.

I was quiet a minute too long for him because he threw his hands up in the air and growled, "See she can't even lay on her back right!"

My mother and sister gasped, while the guys all took a step forward probably planning on coming to my defense, but I'd had enough.

Without thought, I snapped back, "Looks like you don't know me as well as you think. For a matter of fact, I am pregnant."

The room went silent. Every eye turned to me, and I realized what I had done. I knew I wasn't pregnant, or at least not for sure. My cycle was a few weeks away, but they didn't know that, not that my father had bothered to ask.

"You're pregnant?" my father gaped at me.

"Yes," I stated once more, the lie slipping out even easier this time. I avoided the guys' questioning looks as my father began to laugh and crow.

"Finally!" my father shouted, jumping up and down. "An heir! We're saved." He turned to me and gathered me into his arms, hugging me like he used to when I was a small child and hadn't disappointed him. "I'm so proud of you," he murmured in my ear before turning to the men. The smile on his face sank as a frown crept in. "Which one is it? Who's the father?"

Finally, I let my eyes fall on the men who had promised to be by my side every step of the way. Guilt ate at me, but I couldn't stop now. I'd already sunk in too far, might as well bring it home.

"I don't know."

My father's eyes jerked back to mine his brow furrowed in confusion. "What do you mean, you don't know? Which one did you mate with?"

Now, it was my turn to smile, but mine wasn't a nice one. "All of them."

I half-expected the men to jump in and prove I was lying, but none of them said a word. By the slight twitch of their lips, I would be surprised if they hadn't caught on to my ruse. If they hadn't, they weren't going to break my trust now.

My father, however, was a different story. His joy turned to anger as he spun on me.

"Did you do this to spite me? To humiliate me?" he shouted, spittle hitting my face.

I swiped it away with a finger and sneered, "Why so upset? You were the one who told me to screw them both if I wanted to get the job done."

"Dannan!" my mother cried out, mortification on her face. My sister had stayed silent, but I could see the suspicion in her face. I might have fooled our parents, but my sister wasn't buying it.

"What?" my father shot her way. "We needed an heir, but I didn't mean for her to screw him." He gestured violently toward Firestar. "Now, there's an even higher chance we will have to follow through with what our daughter agreed to."

"And what's so wrong with that?" my mother countered. "We are allies. We are supposed to help each other. Lord Amun needs our help."

"Then even more reason to take the advantage now and not promise to help a dying kingdom." My father quickly snapped his mouth closed as he realized what he had said and in front of whom. Composing himself, he cleared his throat and turned away from me. "You are dismissed. We will discuss this later."

"Of course, father." I mockingly bowed at his back before stomping out of the room. I didn't get far before I was cornered by three mountains.

"Can I help you?" I asked with an innocent smile.

"Do you wish to tell us something?" Jack asked with a calm expression. He, of all of them, should be furious since we hadn't had sex yet, but there he was as guarded as ever.

"No, not really." I crossed my arms over my chest, waiting for them to call me out on my bullshit.

"We know you are not pregnant, Maya," Raiden said with a confident tone.

"Do you now?" I cocked a brow at him. "I would think I would know my own body better than you."

Raiden sighed and ran a hand through his hair, "Then we know for sure part of what you said was a lie." His eyes shot over to Jack, who nodded.

They stared at me, waiting for me to break, but they didn't know how determined I was not to give up my hand. My father had used me for his own gain for long enough it was my turn to hold all the cards.

Finally, after I proved I wasn't going to tell them the truth, Firestar said, "Then we best make sure you get to your room comfortably seeing as you are with child and all."

Jack and Raiden exchanged a look with him which made me drop my arms and frown. "What are you talking ab—"

The three of them grabbed me so I was laying longways in their arms. I struggled against them as they walked down the hallway headed toward God only knew where. Finally, when we stopped, they turned me around and blindfolded me.

"What are you guys doing?" I shouted as they took my hands and tied them behind my back. None of them explained what was happening, but then I smelled rain and lightning as a sloppy kiss landed on my right cheek and then hot heat against my left cheek.

"Seriously guys, this isn't funny," I grumbled, pulling against my bindings.

"Do not worry," Jack's voice whispered in my ear. "You are in good hands."

The next thing I knew my feet lifted off the ground, and I was thrown over a shoulder like a sack of potatoes. Jack walked for a few minutes while I fumed, half angry because they had planned this a little too easily and half because I couldn't stare at Jack's butt blindfolded.

A girl's got to have some pleasures in life.

When we finally stopped, the air tensed around us, and a slight wind picked up. Then we were moving again, and that was when I felt it. The ripple of a portal and then the smell of dirt, spoiled food, and people. Lots and lots of people.

"Are we where I think we are?" I asked as Jack

lowered me to the ground. He didn't say anything as he untied my hands and removed my blindfold.

My eyes greedily took in the sight of the concrete and metal buildings around us. The traffic lights were too bright, blocking out any chance of seeing the stars. The sidewalk crowded as the humans rushed about to get to where they were going. I inhaled deeply and sighed.

I was home.

After I had my fill of the surroundings, my gaze landed on Jack. Dressed in a modern style suit, he leaned against a long black limo with a self-satisfied look on his face.

"What is all this?" I asked, glancing away from the limo and to Jack's hopeful face.

"Well," he said, wrapping his arm around my waist. "You have been talking about how you feel overwhelmed by all of us at once."

"But I didn't mean for you to take me away," I interjected with a frown. "What about Raiden and Firestar?"

"Don't worry about them." Jack held the limo door open for me. "We all agreed you needed a break and while you think you hide it well," I opened my mouth to argue with him, but he placed his finger over my lips, "we can tell you actually miss Earth."

I sighed and shrugged. "You got me. Waesigar, while I love it, just doesn't feel like home anymore."

"I know." He gave me a small understanding smile. "That is why we decided it would do you some good to visit Earth again."

I moved closer to the limo standing just inches from Jack. "And you thought you would be the best one to make sure I came back?"

His lips curved into a sly grin as he leaned down as he whispered, "What kind of dragon would I be if I gave up the opportunity to have you all to myself?"

"Not a very good one," I laughed and patted his chest before sliding into the vehicle. "Well, come on then before my father changes his mind."

Jack chuckled and slid in after me. Closing the door behind him, he then wrapped his arm around me. "Tonight, I will show you exactly what being wooed is all about."

Curling into his embrace, the smile on my face making my cheeks hurt, I said, "I can hardly wait."

THANK YOU FOR READING!

Curious about what happens to Maya, Raiden, Jack, and Firestar next?

Find out in Grinding Frost!

AUTHOR'S NOTE

Dear reader, if you REALLY want to read the next Starcrossed Dragons novel- I've got a bit of bad news for you.

Unfortunately, **Amazon will not tell you when the next comes out.**

You'll probably never know about my next books, and you'll be left wondering what happened to Maya and the gang. That's rather terrible.

There is good news though! There are three ways you can find out when the next book is published:

1) You join our mailing list by clicking here.

2) You can also follow Erin on her Facebook Page. We always announce new books in those places as well as interact with fans.

3) You follow us on Amazon. You can do this by going to the store page (or clicking this link) and clicking on the Follow button that is under the author picture on the left side.

If you follow me, Amazon will send you an email when I publish a book. You'll just have to make sure you check the emails they send.

Doing any of these, or all three for best results, will ensure you find out about my next book when it is published.

If you don't, Amazon will never tell you about my next release. Please take a few seconds to do one of these so that you'll be able to join Maya and the gang on their next adventure.

CPSIA information can be obtained
at www.ICGtesting.com
Printed in the USA
BVHW071541211020
591502BV00012BA/882

9 781951 958336